1

2

# Dirty Shorts

**By William Newman**

For Sensei Brian Whitehouse

Copyright © 2019

All incidents and dialogue, and all characters with the exception of some well-known historical figures, are products of the author's imagination and are not to be construed as real. Where real-life historical figures appear, the situations, incidents, and dialogues concerning those persons are entirely fictional and are not intended to depict actual events or to change the entirely fictional nature of the work. In all other respects, any resemblance to actual persons, living or dead, events, or locales is entirely coincidental.


All rights reserved. No part of this publication may be reproduced, distributed, or transmitted in any form or by any means, including photocopying, recording, or other electronic or mechanical methods, without the prior written permission, except in the case of brief quotations embodied in critical reviews and certain other non-commercial uses permitted by copyright law.

Also available by the same author –

The Wizard Trilogy

On Kindle

## 1

There lived in The Kentucky Hills, in Northern-Poland, a legendary creature, some said, an ape-man, some said, a hairy-giant, some said a forest-monster, and others said nothing at all if questioned on the gruesome subject of The Silver Sasquatch. In Conrad Von-Rancour's legendary first book, Claws Of Grisly Glory, he described in detail, with photographs, proof of the creature, he claimed. Back in the 1960's, drugs on the rise, his little book became a world-wide sensation, and thousands of hippys flocked to The Kentucky Hills, in Poland, to search for The Silver Sasquatch, and harvest the incredible magicked-mushrooms, Von-Rancour, wrote about, in much detail, as he himself, became addicted to them during an expedition that would end in bitter tragedy. Von-Rancour, was lucky to make it out alive, he told investigators, when he emerged from the forest that day, the sole survivor, and he would go on to write about it all in his big, weird book, 4.

*

There was once in the Shroom-dream of a young lady, a bright blue Boglin that lived on Mars, it did. It came from outer-space, Cosmia-Gallactic, a wild planet where the humans and their SC Forces, removed many Boglins, including Bluey, as he called himself, in cages to various other locations in Space. Bluey, lost his entire family in the invasion, and though he made it to Mars, only by Space-Pirates, the twisted luck they brought, he also found himself poor, destitute, homeless.

Boglins have always been hated. It is unknown exactly when their Specie began, but it is told by father-boglins, and their grandfathers that the Boglin crawled from the slime one day, from a system, far-removed from our own and *leaking puss from every corner*, said Patrick More, Head-Human-Space-Reporter, in The Space At Night, on tele.

Bright blue *Bluey*, always hated other beings for hating him, and his youth had been a cruel one. Boglins don't go to school, instead, they go to something known as 'Fight Club', where the little ones learn to live, and Bluey, had learned the hard way.

Pink Professor Humankind, at fight school, told him he had promise, but that he lacked common-sense or discipline, which Humankind, had moaned a lot about in lectures repeatedly; The Stupidity of Boglins, those lectures were titled, and caused some outrage, although most Boglins were either too drunk, eating or mating to care, all the time. Fight Club, in recent Boglin-Years, has become more of a meat-market, Humankind, itself, professing to believe that their specie had *de*volved. This saddened the intellectual-community of the Boglins, who tried hard to build relations with other species, their own had offended over the space-years, and failed. The intellectual ones were often considered worse than the usual, regular stupid type, who were to a degree harmless in their scathing criticisms and moaning about everything in the universe. The Boglin Has Found Voice! Declared popular magazine, *National Universe*, some decades ago, and since then they have been growling louder than ever!

Bluey, was part of the most recent growl- a growl against SC, and everything else, as usual. "And now I live with a tramp!" Moaned Bluey, snuggled in his master's pocket by the entrance of the subway station.

Mars City Central.

"A fucking *shit-hole!*" said Blue, looking up at his sleeping, bearded drunk master, woollen hat, *mangy* beard. "Rat for dinner! Rat for lunch! Shit-flakes for breakfast, covered in rain! I'm gonna' jump-shit-ship, By Godlin!" he whined.

Godlin was the God of Boglins.

Quiet, *its* voice remained to poor Bluey, his pocket.

\*

"*One of the greatest things in life is an Indian takeaway*, I told my boss. She told me that crisp packets were to be washed and put in a special bin, from now on. I had looked at her sideways, the expression between professionals where the words should be uttered, but are not- instead, a look. The look. *Just do it!* She said, heeling in a semi-circle and marching away, those clacking heels."

The Doctor regards me sternly. "Are you working too much again?" she asks.

"Probably."

"Tell me more about the dreams."

Way down in busy Utunga City Central streets- cars, buses, bikes make their noises, people go by in droves. Up here, in Doctor Singleton's office, I am shielded from all that, at the moment, her soft leathery recliner. "Tell me about the Bigfoot."

I look at her, weary with Bigfoot. Weary with my addiction to Silver Sasquatch, the best of the *Sh*-rooms, even Jim Carey has his grinning mug on the packet, giving it two-thumbs up. On other packets there are portraits of other celebrity Sasquatch users, Terrence McKenna and mellow-fellow-fro'-landscape-zen-artist, Bob Hope, arm in arm. I collect the shroom-packets, or *shooting pouches*, as they are called and I have many. The current packet I have has a picture of Grimace, on it from McDonald's, which is odd and makes no sense, but I like his pretty purple fur and mischief, his big eyes pill-box red, half-munched shrooms falling from his flappy mouth. "I don't want to speak of the Bigfoot," I tell her, seriously. "Every time I speak of the Bigfoot, *Silver*, I go there, that weird Polish forest, and her, The Muffin-Top Queen, her friend, Frog, Blue-Boglin and Mountain Man. It is too strange a world!" I tell her. "And King-Buzzsaw plays an electric guitar there, while a Count flaps his wings. The scream of a banshee, the howl of a Bigfoot!"

"It's Ok, we can take a rest."

"Silver never rests!" I glare at her, alarming her. "And he is angry!"

"*He?*" she asks me.

"He." I tell her. "A Great-White Sasquatch!"

\*

Earth
Africa

Utunga

Quentin Seagull, sat quietly wondering at the beach. He stroked his long, bright-white beard with a slender ageing man's hand, a wry-smile, two bright-blue eyes that marvelled oval at the sky where seagulls swirled and one or two died. They were pink, those gulls, bright-pink, and Q, as he called himself, marvelled not only at the sky, but at the effect *Crunk* -a bright-white-pill- had had on him this very Monday morning and a dead fallen pink seagull on his table that only he saw, he knew. "Extraordinary!" he uttered, as the people around him at Le Strip Tease, gathered for the regular mid-morning break, chat and refreshments of ordinary.

The Wizard, had been here, he knew. "Albert! That wily wizard!" he reminded himself, wondering which of the cocktails the old, *old* man would have chosen? "A pink one, certainly," he decided, *sure*, running a long finger down the laminated sheet of *Menu*, admiring the vast choice of drinks available.

\*

This was Q's first time on the African island, *Utunga*, miles from anywhere, certainly the *mainland*, wherever that was, he had come from, a connecting private flight, and a place he was suitably familiar with.

Beings of his rank, generally were.

"A puce one!" he was certain, tapping his finger on it, Tickled Pink, a little photo, a dead seagull and tickled pink he felt suddenly, *knowing again, that...*

An empty Coke can rattled under his seat in the breeze, reminded him suddenly of his odd, recent *rattling* mind, keeping him awake for long, meditative, and oddly dark hours since he arrived here, whenever that was, *long ago?* Time was a factor that slipped in and out of Q's cosmic life of a different time. "What peace can become of this?" he asks himself quietly, some sincerity, changing his mood, feeling it change, feeling it all change, letting it slip, slide; crossing his legs, lighting his pipe, watching the smoke catch the brisk sea-breeze, coming brisk on-shore from the turquoise ocean, a crow's flap just across the golden sand beach beyond Le Tease, Le Strip. "The wizard's favourite holiday spot!" he reminds himself, drooling, remembering Mad Wolf, a Mad *Warlock*, Druid or *something* who was murdered here, there, *everywhere.* "1999," Q, reminds himself, darkly, and in a sullen whisper. "Chalk it up. And, if you don't believe that..."

\*

*The day shall be long today*, he suspects, as the days tend to be here on Ut*i*nga. "Where things move slow, and life can be cheap, or very expensive. Always *very*," he utters, contemplatively, softly now, as the waitress, a large, pretty black woman, who looks bothered, approaches his table, one of many down her long list of happy customers on the terrace that Monday, *Monday* morning.

"Yes sir?" she asks him, barely noticing him, *breaking* him it seems, then glancing his startling white beard, slim-grin; it seems to excite something good within her anyway and her brown eyes twinkle with unfounded delight.

"You don't see many beards here on the island?" Q, asks her, smiling deeper, a gentle, familiar evince that brings instant reciprocation all over.

"Not really."
"Well, I'll try the Tickled Pink."
"Good choice, sir!"

\*

A cargo ship arrives slowly on the horizon as *I* wait to be

Tickled Pink. I watch her steel bulk form, *assemble* in the heat-hazy skyline where there is a stampede of bleach white horses, reminding me of Poems Dedicated To The Sea, a slim tome *he* picked up on Mars, the strangest of little bookshops *he* found one night whilst on a secret mission in The Underfoot Arena Department of *MCC*. "MCC. Mars City Central. And from which ravaged shore has this heavy load come from?" I ask myself, the sounds of the shoreline washing away last night's bad dreams, visions, the smell of fresh coffee, *he*, the unwanted attention of cigarettes and caramel waffles, reassuring as Time finds 11.06AM.

"Right on time!" I say, feeling somewhat odd about the dark-spell those three words hold deep within, *here*, right under the surface of all of this mess, cast, where I dwell often, like the witches and wizards, do, it must be said. "Right on time?" And then, my Tickled Pink, arrives, as if heeding my eponymous phrase, yet impatient I am not, hence, a slight dark-awkwardness as this long, puce-pink drink, of much alcoholic content, I am advised, finds me quickly with bitter blood-mango sweetness, received with pleasure by throat.

*I like slow*, I remember, the crunk definitely doing something.

"The Shadow?" I utter, watching the black lady, her tray of drinks for clients, *feeling him*, too. He is gone from here, now, though. He would be of no use on this mission.

*Mission?*
*Mere shadows of the blue.*

\*

As someone of The Sacred Seagull Clan, a man who was to *become*, no less, he wondered about the sentiment that his visit here in any way could be categorized as *mission*. Deep-discernment was one of Q's blessings and curses. *Life is a mission sir, yet, there is no purpose.* A wizard, Albert The Sad, reminds him, in memory, as a ghost, from a shady, perfect black-cosy corner of this very terrace, and Q, stifles unfounded laughter. "That *damn* wizard!" he mused, in the past, now, removed the little, orange-patterned paper-umbrella, from his drink, then put his beardy-bright lips to the pink-stripy straw, looking down his long nose, or *beak*, as Oysters called it as they went passed him, for someone, and the pink, zesty flavour tickled him, very pill pink. "Pink seagulls," he said, flabbergasted. "Reproduction?"

\*

"Sid, this shit's sick, dude," I say, calmly, passing the joint to black Rat, behind his drums, poised, ready for a hit after another foul day of Max, Rad Stallion. Yet, *he* is also stoned now, calmed, Max Silvers, after calling us, like his audience, once or twice, cunts and maggots, and Sally Doll, my new girlfriend is here too, tonight, skanking our weed.

She's a foul bitch, is ol Sal'. She's already pissed on me carpet, twice, whispered "rape" tenderly in my ear as she made first date sex with me I practically forgot, as I got hideously wrecked on red-wine at the Indian, out of fear of first-date, Sally Doll, of newly-signed Barbie Rape Doll.

My heart is beating abnormally fast, my arsehole still tickling after the ridiculously hot curry I ordered, for the fuck of it, as I was already very drunk before I even found restaurant. The fucking quality of dope these days is literally worth the over-used word awesome. *Those bligythy youths*, I think, really fucking, fuckibng

high

<u>a river of sound</u>
a tribute to The Doors

poetry is close to music
a state of mind
hypnotic
free
subconscious goes
get up

recite
they
I find it security
music
projecting
nothing political
dug it
the kids
and
religious
people stations
assemblage
masses of yeast
feast
communion and energy
no reason
no reason
no reason

it's a funny thing
it's ours too
small
a shaman
of all the ages
a question of a psychological omen

love me
it'll be alright

*

"The Screaming Ghouls is a great name for the second album," I tell Max with red-wine high-point authenticity, before it all goes down the dreaded tanin-helter-skelter and familiar depression at the bottom. "I've been having nightmares about them, under post-apocalyptic skies, purple and evil- and then I've woken up next to Sally, that mop of blond hair, like Gladys' mop-end, after she's bleached the floors at night." I shudder. "She sleeps with her eyes open, too, does Sal'!"

"The screaming ghouls," he utters, his black-strat, in lap, buzzing with destruction. "What does Sid say about it?" he asks.

"Sid's been away, in Germany, cashing in over the summer beer-festivals with new *pal* Peter, as Brian, told me. I don't really care what Sid says, to be honest, and Brian's jealous- and Sid's still yet to respond to Huffstuffingpuff's list of complaints!"

"You can't complain about the album, Joe," Max, rightly tells me, and it's true- *Shitty Litter*, is a damn good debut. Reviews prove that statement, despite the fact my red-wine drinking has escalated furiously in the weeks since Litter's release onto the scene and the attention it is getting, especially in Germany!

*Those metal-mad Germans!*

The kids love it! As do legendary *Rim-stein*, we are told.

I feel like a fucking Nazi-paedo, and with the added weight around my belt, as a white-trash over-privileged white-wino's pale hairy-gut spills over, I admire drummer-Rat, who maintains his weight and Bruce Lee muscles via a strict regime of mostly hard drugs, violent-fasting and a genuine professional musician's dedication to his craft, like Lee. Rarely do you see him far from his drum-stall, like you never saw Bruce, far from a Dojo, and today is no exception as he lurks there, not Bruce, but Rat, in the dimmest lighting of our rehearsal and practice room here at Nasty

Fucking Records, *LAS Alberto!*
*Our Dojo!*

I come over all dizzy again with too much excitement as I eye black Rat, waiting to bash again- waiting for the signal from Chief Mad Max, who brought us something very special with his diabolic power-riffs on the new B-Side, Dank Axe, that should, in hindsight have been the A-Side.

"Hindsight really is a matted, hairy cunt!" was Sid's excuse, in a heated meeting, down the local, a place where all the old punks, skaters and metlers have washed up in uneasy, yet grateful years, as good things like friendship, and good pint prices take the sting out of heavy drinking and *bad-back's* cold, social reality.

"That is true, Sid," I responded, firmly, virtually a bowl-full of throat-scour-red wine, the glasses are that fucking large in there as they *modernise! More air does piss make taste better.* "*But!* Dare I question, that *old*-Brian, bless his heart, may have finally lost his ear for a hit? *Axe* is better than the A, *Carnage!*"

Sid, had bobbed his head, rolled his big eyeball, hit-up Mr Fist, said "*Aww!*"; he knew it. Brian Whitehorse, was glue. Even Sid, had to admit that it was *he*, not Brian, this time, who noticed Barbie Rape Doll, in-fact, Brian, as I recall, and told Sid, called them, and I quote- *talentless sluts who could use another raping!* "Despicable!" I had told Sid, ratting Brian out the very day after the comment without concern after his *rape joke*, as I called it, saying it upset Sally, and it did a bit. "He's lost it, Sid!" I had said, callously, that night in the pub white-knighting like a total tosser. "Whitehorse is ready for the glue pot!"

Sadly, a few weeks into the future, it would be Brian, who, having found out about the callous remarks I had made, and having been sacked, though gently, by Sid, had had the last laugh, *heh* did- smashed the back window of my deep-purple, lowered Golf- got in, had a shit.

For a while, I wasn't exactly sure it was Brian, until the CCTV footage surfaced, under my father's supervision after I bothered him- it made for an amusing video, even I had to admit after several viewings; old Brian, shaking a leg, cricket bat- we would use some frames in our next video, Dank Axe, where we dressed Max, as a Barbarian Over-Lord, and I wore a Spinal Tap T-Shirt, to take the edge off of the dark, satanic chords that that song *spat* as crazy old, Brian Whitehorse *shat*

-*out* dank manure on my back seats that night in wicked glee.

It was massive! Not the shit, the second album. Well, relatively. I tell people that it put metal back on the map anyway! And, under the relatively useless wing of old Sid Nasty, we almost embarked on a plane with Barbie Rape Doll, their new album, Teenage Fuck Nugget, also successful, on a *Fucking Excuse For A World Tour*, as Nasty, his new assistant, Peter Doughhatty, a dishevelled but youngish, brilliant floppy-haired-failed-hipstar, with a real, real drug problem, almost came too, after his missus, Backy Wackyblack, snuffed it, called it no-no in rehab.

\*

The Blue-Vein Boy, is a dark interlude-song, dedicated to the poor lad who tragically lost his life in The Meat Factory, or whatever that damn place was called!

Not young scamp*star* Doughhatty!

What a night that was!

One to remember!

The meat pie factory disco.

After much generosity by his very own devilish best friend, Mr Fist, Sid, indeed, clambered up onto the stage, the bouncers distracted as the Paramedics arrived for the lad at the bar with us, dead indeed, by overdose via his penis-vein, *gone with the blue*, as the addicts apparently call it. As he hoisted his very expensive trade-mark sheepskin coat, Max, Rat, and many, many horrid others cheered and saluted their drinks, as ageing Sid, his pink-strip, released his sloppy brown payload onto the corner of the stage.

As they carried the dead chap out on a stretcher, I wondered which incident was more horrible in that instant in the pie-hole- Sid's dripping shit gravy, or underage overdose via the dick?

*Both, were and always will be bad things to see on a night out*, I concluded, days later in the bubble-bath.

\*

Hi!

I'm really, truly glad you're doing OK. The job sounds very promising and I truly wish it to be everything you want. You're a very talented little Virgo, a powerhouse indeed and deserve the best. And little Pouch, her bit of grass, bless her hairy heart :)

As for me, well, after the intense attempts at manipulation, control and desperate to prove me to be a 'bad boy' the last year or so, I had no other option but to walk from my job.

And once again I find myself drained and broke!

I will be signing-on, Monday.
But, as I cried last week in the drizzle, top car park, an old misery creeping back in, I realised that I am worth more than that horrible place and their evil, wicked managers- and some staff, and kicked that shit feeling right out!

My dream, is that my writing abilities -books etc- are recognised somewhere, by someone. I want to be a writer. I am a very good writer. I don't fit into this society, and they don't want me -the real me-, so I will be a recluse until I can either find a writing job worthy, or am collected to go and write dark comedy for TV or something.

I want a wife.
I want a kid.
A decent income.
And I want a home I can call my own.

And I feel I deserve this peace.

Of course, I will go along with all divorce procedures, and thank you for dealing with it.

If, one day I get somewhere in life financially, you will be handsomely rewarded. And that is a promise I intend to keep.

My parents are actually being quite supportive at the mo, having witnessed, since my return my despair, frustration and determination to succeed, so that's something. They have no reason to be horrible to me anyway- I have been nothing but supportive, positive, kind and invested in betterment of people's lives, but right now..

I'm out.
And that is what they deserve.

I want what I deserve.
And I deserve a break.
God help me.

*Thank you.*

<u>Count and Countess</u>

She's right here
but what a scene
right there
a warm glare!
she's everywhere
everyone


and the men in rags opened the tortoise like a fray-benthos pie
and in that can, blubber, whitish blubber
they will put upon their barbecues
as the women cut off a woman's breasts
and the men, remove a white-trash penis.

He showed me a chainsaw beheading
at three in the morning
blamed it on me
blamed it on his friendships we watched the
whoring blades of the executors saw
rapidly
remove those terrified heads.
But that is the wicked and legendary way of the count

beware those wings
font make them flap

> they have put tears in the eyes of hero
> and made rich men poor
>
> like a gay batman he soars in the ink black nights
> his coffin full of cobwebs and video games
> nasty surprises
> like frank
> and in the heart of it all, his wicked black queen of hearts
> his diabetic countess
> loved by all.
> Together, they, the black hours, rule.

\*

"Yeah, well," says white-South African human of origin, now Mayor of Mars City Central, to his entourage at the bar. His PA, Amanda, waits patiently next to him, glasses on. "I hit the darky wid me jeep! *Ye!* Were hurtlin' thryu the bush an out *e'* pooped like, bounced r*ii*ght off me bonnet, the crazy kafa! Ran reet off back int' bush he did," he says, beaming, very drunk, accent full-on. "An I musta whacked im judging by the dent he left, the nutta!"

"South Africa sounds wonderful, Tool," says some politician, blue, a big cigar.

"*Yee* it is!" he rambles on, secretly missing Earth after recently losing a foot in a heavy drinking competition with bad-boy Beadle. His big, bandaged new foot rests up on a poof. "We got *Oo*striges, Table-Top-Mountain and the big, buxom women, who love a little o' the ol' one in the bum," he giggles, wiggling his finger. "It's paradise *id* is!" he reminisces, grinning ear to ear.

\*

One day, Brat Anderson, formerly of brilliance, Suede, came in, pale-faced, looking for Sid, a fix of nasty.

"Upstairs with Doughhatty, cooking-up," I told Brat, moodily.

"You look like shit mate!" Brat, told me.

"Yerself mate!" I told him, shuffling back into my corner of reception with my bottle. "The Tears!" I called out after him. "Tears of fucking shame!" I heckled him, in secret hero-worship, remembering queuing, also as a lonely YA, for a copy of Nude. One of my favourite albums, for a while, until I remembered that you *can not kill the metal*, I will tell Brat, later, when he has cooked-up, is warmer, safer, and I might be able to get into his mysterious life in the streets, avoiding Suede.

*Re-union, bitch!* I will tell him later. *One more album then an overdose*, I will suggest, giving him the wink and getting my own back on those wimpy tears.

The dreams, yes, the dreams may have been bad, wild, ugly, pretty, painful and always very terrible and often crushing, but I feel slightly more purified now, especially after laying off of the red wine the last few weeks, about half way on our second album, The Screaming Ghouls, third song *Donkey Kong* just about ready for the dirty polish of new technician Peter Doughhatty, who has proved himself worth the high price-tag he carries, despite his bum ways. "I still miss Wackyblack," he told us, tears in his eyes, every fucking night after shooting up again, encouraged by Sid.

"Momma ain't coming back from Rehab, Pete, ye fkin' Babyshambles!" Max told him angrily, after losing his temper finally. "She said no no no! And so do I!"

Speaking of women of rock, singer, guitarist, Sally Doll, is still my girlfriend, although I don't see her very often as she ghosts me *in spite* all the time. She's more love-less than the legendary hole, herself, *ol' Courtney!* Sally's still angry I cancelled the ridiculous world-tour, mad Sid, had *pepped* on my father's money, the tosser! So, I cancelled the lot, and have slowed down recording of the album to ensure missing Sid's greedy deadline! We all still hang out at the studio, but the atmosphere is tense, dreadful, touch and go.

Max, has taken to long hours of Mario-Kart, wide-eyed as the LSD drives his psychedelic Kart home night after night, day after day! Rarely does he emerge from his *study*, as he calls it.

Rat, lurks and sleeps in the corner near his kit, listening to his Walkman, sometimes cruising bare chested around the corridors of Nasty Fucking Records, on his roller-skates, big J-dummy on, and overall, I find that the whole ambiance, as new-needed Security, outside, wallow, as it snows for January, we inside, are living the middle part of The Thing.

The question is, then, at this odd interlude of our dark career- *which of us has it got to?*

All of us, I think, shivering, paranoid, nervous. *We are all The Thing*, I consider sensing inevitable death. *And Hole were better than Nirvana*, I am forced to admit, finally in my loneliness. *Those sneaky bitches!*

*Oh*, and as a YA, I remember- I *didn't* have a U2 poster, but I did paint a giant face of Bono onto my black, semen-splashed walls. Then painted over it in black when he didn't answer the letter I wrote him, asking if I could hang out with the band, get some tips from Adam, and complementing them on their Zoo TV thing, Bono's look at that point etc. *Don't get me started on Mephisto!* I would write to him now, if I could be even remotely bothered.

\*

"Donkey Kong is about a circus monkey with secret alcohol and depression issues," I tell the woman from Time Off! "Isn't Wilf Wilson available?" I ask her.

She gives me a look. "Sexual harassment scandal, part of the #tometoyou craze."

"Oh."

"Were you all on drugs and alcohol during Shitty Litter?" she asks.

"Oh yeah."

"What's it like working with Sid Nasty? You've been together for a few years now?"

"Nearly two. And it's hell, love, honestly!"

"Why?"

"Well, he's a good guy, but a fucking nut-job, a raver! At his age! I tell him."

"Rumours say he's back on the needle?"

"Oh yeah!"

"And Peter Doughhatty, his producer?"

"High as a paper-thin kite, darling!"

\*

The white wolf runs down the crack in the jagged cliff. He can see the plump white seagull in the near distance, perched as it is and he could use the meal. The road here has been long, dangerous; once or twice the mad wolf lost his way on the path, was killed, re-born, and how many centuries it took the slender beast to get here was untold. The only indication of those long years were the wolf's many stripes and markings, from beige, cream to bright white; this Wolf had earned its stripes-

And deserved the seagull.

I wake up, groan, open eyes. In the far/near distance I can hear Max's Fender giving it growl. "At-least he's practising again," I remind myself, wondering how much more of this rock and roll lifestyle I want to live, to be honest.

Another hangover. Another wasted night, with nightmares-

Wolves, this time.

No, *Wolf.*

Singular.

\*

"Can I get a fry-up Gladys?" I ask her, seating myself alone with the newspapers- glad, so glad of coffee, peace.

"How do you want it?" she asks.

"The works," I tell her.

There are a few people in the mini-cafeteria today, from media, techs, musicians, and, "Sally Doll!" I sigh, as she comes striding in, looking very unhappy. She comes right over to my table, hits me with it.

"I'm pregnant!" she grins, but a devil's dark twinkle in her eyes that suggests something far-removed from joy.

"Oh. That's nice," I smile, feeling strangely empty inside. *Perhaps it is the same numbing shock one has in such things as car crashes?* I wonder.

"Is that it?" she snaps. "Is that all you got?"

"Isn't one enough, Sal?" And she punches me, square in the face, sending me backwards over my chair.

"Get up Giblet!" she beckons me. "Get up so I can give you another one!" she shouts at me, echoing in the hushed astonishment.

"Fuck off!" I dare, and feel the pointed, steel tip of her long PVC boot find my stomach, cruel.

"Have that for breakfast, you fat cunt!" she tells me.

\*

Back in the studio, still reeling from breakfast, the added hate Gladys gave me with my food, deep-bruising and revelations of unwanted fatherhood.

"Brighton's sweet mate," says Doughhatty, doing his hair in the mirror he has propped over the mixing desk. It's not so much that Peter loves himself; he uses more the mirror to cut and consume drugs.

"I don't like Brighton," moans Max. "Last time I was there I ended up sleeping in a bedroom that stank of curry all night."

Sid, giggles, his eyes retracted at this time due to heroin. His eyes are narrow, dark, *dark* slits.

"I got a hotel there!" Pete gloats. "The Doughhatty! Me and me mates run it, it's wild mate!"

"A bunch of cry-baby libertines all shacked up, charging rent for a night in a room next to you lot while you all get jacked up and write poetry!" Max gives him. "Mad as a Hatty to stay there for a night!" he slams.

*

"Tell me me more about the incident at Letticesphere Festival, Joe? What happened that day?"

"Do I have to?"

"Please!" she beckons, a beautiful smile I cave-in to immediately. "*Well.* The traffic getting out was shit so I took a shit on the toilet. Not in it. On it. Then we watched innocent people recoil in Joy, in our car, in the traffic that didn't fucking move for hours!" I explain, angrily topping up my glass. "A right shambles! I had to do something to take the edge off of the tension in the car that day. Max was ready to commit actual murder, and my girlfriend at the time, a crazy frog, kept taunting me! Shit was bound to happen!"

*

"Do you want more eggs on your toast?" Max, mocks me.

Gladys, scowls. She has the face of a real witch, and I fear she is casting another hate-spell on me, I shall fight with more red-wine, later. "Proud of yourself? Getting Sal up the duff! That's your little grown baby-man's dream over mate!" she points at me, firing a cruel, long one up. "Next time you put your little dick in a hole, make sure it's bagged, *long-hair!* Anyway, how about 18 years baby jail for dessert tonight?" she cackles, waving her fag-wand at me, as Max and Rat burst into laughter, at my very expense.

\*

"Come on baby," Sally whispers to me in my nightmare, that night. "Come on baby," she whispers, as she thrusts herself on me, unwillingly, each. My new Jack In The Box, just for me, my dick on a spring.

My box is pitch-black, shiny, cold and unbreakable, unlike Rhianna's, who I suggest has a part to play in this, somehow, the worst nightmare I have ever had as the sounds of screaming children *echo* in the gloom.

"Stop it, Sally," I urge her, unable to resist her moist hole that has me. Her hot, pale mass, slippery and heavy. "STOP IT" I scream, waking myself up, covered in sweat, gasping for air, begging for death.

## The Drained Room

Once Upon A fallen night-club
the club of the night no one here *tone*
in a place where nothing exists
nothing, no, *not at all.*
Not even a telephone.
There are the bunkum crusts of pizzas here
clues of citizenry, the spillage of beer
and as no one looks harder there is nothing
here in the empty room, after all.
*suggestion*
The spatial relation whispers..


*admirer*
*Stare at me with empty eyes*
*I can see beyond those lies*
masses of black stuffed-crust
and then my empty room will be replete with dusk
that burning husk
caught in a glare, *glance*
one ball-and-socket chance, one flicker,
the shadows of many, the yarn dance
the dusk, empurpled now, thicker
the fire lasted only once.

*smile at me like you care*
*allow me to wonder, stare*
masses of black stuffed-crust
fills, floats random in the air
the callous dust.

*Do you feel for this life?*
You may feel like asking
the empty room has only vacuous answer
no one affair left to feel.

Stars aspect down unto my eyes
I look up onto their closed book
through the big hole in the ceiling of the empty room
where no one is there, no coats on the coat hooks
I bespeak no one, the only incomparable in the room
hoping soon, the motivation of hope will too subside
without word, suchlike the tide, and I also.. quickly die

\*

Black hours, days later, I find myself in Sid's office; there is a photograph of Figgy Shitdust, on his desk in a nice frame. Figgy, has his usual lightning bolt painted on his face, that puffy white hair, silver jump suit. "Didn't Bowie threaten Shitdust, for copying Stardust?"

"As I told Bowie!" Sid pumps-up, rare motion from him considering his recent heroin. "Shitdust's the yang to your Stardust's yin, I told him!"

Doughhatty giggles.

"He took it well, and everyone was a bit scared of big-bosses The Queen, back then, ol' Fred, his violent mood-swings, Brian May-Or-May-Not, as he was known- an' they liked Shitdust, to be honest. Fred, said Shitdust cheered him up when he felt suicidal, like a king's jester! Ha!"

I turn to smile at Sally. She glares at me. "Maybe we could call our child Freddy?" I say, finding pitch-perfect fake-enthusiasm *tone*, trying to soften her constant temper.

"Fuck off!" she tells me as Doughhatty chokes on his new crack-pipe for laughing as snow outside turns to wild torrential rain.

\*

Taking a long walk along The River Dismal, the drizzle, grey, austere skies of early year here in Ol' London wrap around me. Wrapped in my raincoat, hat, scarf, gloves, I feel old. There was once a time, the young Joe Giblet, would have braved this weather in his usual T-Shirt, Jeans, back, forth to the pub in the evenings, long periods of never going out, or anywhere at all, sometimes. Huffpuffingstuff didn't care! He was too busy on his own path of wreckage to consider his bastard loser son's misery as a wealthy, lonely young adult, *I was!* I whine to myself as a boat sounds its weary fog-horn.

*Oh, The River!*

How many bodies have walked this weary Sunday walk, considered throwing themselves in, as the rain worsens in a flurry and seagulls peck at floating matter? I can almost feel the deep, drop-down rumblings of my thick bass-strings as my mind wanders *down-*

down with the river-sea of shit, shit brown.

I drown.

Sally Doll, should be on my arm this afternoon! I consider,

unsure, growing angry instead of melancholy. What have I done that was *soo* wrong? I wonder, wishing this relationship with Barbie Rape Doll, never started! Aside from the fact they are very good, their new album, Teenage Fuck Nugget, a real foot-tapper, the girls, particularly Sally, have the worst attitudes towards everything I have ever seen. And I thought Max, Sid, Doughhatty, their chums were obnoxious!

And now, I'm having a baby with their psychotic lead singer, Sal. *How the willow weeps!* I despair, certainly not aloud, as rough looking chavs pass, yet, sensing, somehow, somewhere, deep, dark, that I may be in *very love with her*, as Huffstuffingpuff, warned me I may feel about a woman one day if I am unlucky.

"And, we all got unlucky," he glared at me that day, his purple nose.

"But I've been in love," I tell myself, "and I drank myself out of it."

"That wasn't love," *Puffy* told me, the tosser, I remember. "That was your penis, boy," he told me, and I didn't believe him, then. Now, maybe, I do, and shall consider spending more time with old Puffy, as it seems he may have cared, or at-least had some slim interest in me, his only son -apart from two others- after all.

\*

"Look, I'm not interested, Joe!" she *yells* me, sullen. It rains outside the Hey!Hey!O'ilay! restaurant chain we eat at, an argument over *I-Tie, Diego, Wop or Chinky*, as potty-mouth Southern commoner, Sally said, and, *Oh*, how it rains.

"Would you like a dough-ball? Great with the garlic butter!" I poke one at her across the table.

"I don't know how you can eat that shit!" she tells me, batting it onto the floor, her make-up severe this evening, I notice as *ball* finds couple seated nearby. Sorry, I nearly tell them, but Crunked,

I yell-

"It's Italian! Everyone loves Italian!"

"Not everyone likes garlic!" she yells back, and things go hushed, *loory*, waiter's eyes burn, and I almost make a Vampiress Joke, concerning garlic, restrain, remembering her wicked pointy goth-boots that could easily reach me under this two-seater, my delicate shins. "And I was talking about you! Your *pig* attitude!" she rants on loud. "I'm pregnant, and *you* don't care!"

"I care, Sally," I say, calmly, mouth full of lovely dough and butter. Helping it down with a large swig of red, red wine, I gulp- "I've already agreed to finance *it*, and well, I love you."

She smiles, I relax. "You mean that?"

"Yes," I say, seeing two of her. "Have you decided what Pizza you'll be having?" I ask her, attempting to move the conversation, hoping she likes Pizza. *I've never had Pizza*, she told me, earlier. *Who has never had Pizza?* I wondered, red-flags flapping wildly all over the place as we entered this territory of attempted reconcile, where other sharp women also interview their men over food, for faults, and make them pay for it. I miss the good old days, the simple old days, a bag of chips, ice-cream and a walk by the windy ocean, or a drive out to the country, pretend it's nice, get drunk anyway, get the coitus done then get home quickly to the warmth, comfort and safety of the tele, forever.

Instead, it is this.

## TWO

Sunny Beach, is the name of a coastal town up north. Seven miles north of Brainchester, its Gothic University, and home of The legendary *Plum Baron*, SB, is a solitary, run-down, yet geographically, rather rugged and pretty place, with a host of local people, and many, many skeletons. Old *Skeleton-Billy*, himself, said it was a pretty average place to live; that was before he was dragged-out to sea by a dreaded *ripe-tide* on a nude-new-years-day swim; Saggy Alice, as she was known, found him, washed up on the rocks two days later, or rather her dog did as it pecked at the remains. *Murder!* She would scream, but then, she was known for that, although, murder, indeed, would be on the menu, as eccentric old, Saggy Alice, was found hung in her stately home up on the cliff. And so, the sun of the beach, often went behind dark clouds with such drama, that gave the folk something to do and think about, and talk and gossip about as they met daily in town for coffee, Gin and much beer. It was your typical seaside town, in verity, despite the crumbling Skeletons family and unusually high number of heroin users, *but* it was when the slimy semi-skeleton of a real sea-monster washed up on Sunny Beach, one day, that locals wondered if the hallo-weed legends of grisly *Morgwar*, were real...

\*

   I, Clarence Nutkins Skeletons, am a writer, I am. I live with my mother. It was I who ranted to the Virgo, I did, whining about leaving my job, as a shelf-filler, and whining generally about my cruel life.
   She ignored my letter, as always. And being a black-butterfly,

of an emo, and an actor, I cried about that too.

Let me tell you about my sad, sorry life here at Sunny Beach. In-fact, let me cry you a river..

*

I always wanted to be David Bowie, instead, I ended up more like *moody*-Numan, worse. As a child I wanted to be a magician, would perform magic tricks for my so-called friends, who would, after allowing me my range of limited tricks, bought in a handy box, turned on me and called me the village idiot. "This isn't a village!" I had retaliated. They threw mayonnaise at me anyway, and laughed me into a dirty corner near an old brick shed. In that shed, having clawed, wriggled my way inside like a worm, through desperation to escape them, I found a copy of MNE, and so began my desire to become David Bowie. Later, as my struggles continued, record collection and poetry books mounted, the same long-line at the job-centre, mother getting older, meaner, I would move into acting inspired by Mad Mel Gibson, whom I always felt got a bad wrap! The cheeseburger thing actually made me crack a smile, and his hand-puppet film made me feel almost grateful to be me. My first performance at The Sunny Beach Theatre, Shakespeare's Macbeth, was a disaster. In my fear of the stony audience, I bottled-it and ran! One of the other actors in Act 2, did the same, making me feel better as I shivered, in fetal-shame, at home, having lied to my mother, telling her it was all a total success.

She would find out. She always did! And have her revenge on me too, she would, allowing father to move back in, inviting the havoc and filth. She knew, even though I am nearly forty, that Big Jim, or *Daddio*, as she called him, would beat me for being bad, weedy, an artist, and a failure!

She knew, I write, as I cry, listening to Bauhaus, remembering better days, when I was skinnier, paler, more socially interesting, less bullied. That bitch knew that drunk, drunk father would gaslight, bully and hate on me, and make my already difficult life here at Sunny Beach, Hell.

She Knew.

\*

Father pissed himself on the couch the first night he arrived. "You're a f*oo*kin' fag!" he told me, as he fell in through the door, carrier-bag of wares and a rotten stench of cigarettes, alcohol. His vest was stained, as always, his chubby-armpits hairy, and as he fell straight into the sofa, slinging his muddy trainers onto the coffee-table, mother's precious coffee-table, her mother's, my grandmother's, I knew there was going to be trouble.

"Where's yer mother?" he asked, finding a pack.

"Give me one of those!" I demanded. "In the kitchen, baking cookies! Can't you smell them?"

"The only thing I can smell, lad, is the dog-shit I just walked in'*t* carpet!" he sniggered, reaching into his bag for a can of 888, cracking it. "*Aye!* The Chuckle Brothers are on! *T'me, t'yuu!* Ha! Love it! Here, Clarence, ye fag, go get mummy, tell her Daddio's here!" he chuckles- "Tell her *t'* get kit off!" he says, spilling more lager down his vest.

\*

He was always a bastard, Big Jim Skeletons! As a youth, he stole one of my favourite books by Charles Bukowski, read it, out of spite, then *inspired* made me cut the grass using scissors. When I refused, he got drunk, then came up to my room that night dressed as a clown wielding a meat-cleaver! I screamed in terror, as he hacked at my door.

Mother found me, huddled in a corner of my black bedroom, having wet my pants, and she threw that very book at me, angrily, for waking her up, she said, as the spine bounced off my head, and- *giving your dad bad ideas!*

For my fifth birthday he strapped fireworks to me and told me to run through a bonfire, laughing and jeering with his drunken mates, mother, hers. I nearly did, too, so I am told, before I was rescued by the sympathetic neighbour, who would attempt to rape me as a schoolboy, I shall add!

*What a bastard!* I consider, sat at the beach, on a big rock, wondering about Sandy, my last and only wife.

"Oh, Sandy," I utter, watching seagulls swirl. "She can kiss my dick too!" I say, knowing she wouldn't, now. Now, she has another dick to kiss- a big, black one. Maybe she will throw her empty dinner-plate at him, like I did her having been goaded? I wonder, curling my thinning hair with a finger. Dangerously thinning, it hits me again, wondering when my order for hair-restoration cream will arrive as I get dangerously low in the bathroom, or *Pharmacy. Maybe this new big black fella is getting it worse than me?* I wonder, almost finding a smile, instead the grey, brown sea tumbles down from the north, like shit, and my remaining mid-morning morale plummets as the rain-drops dash *cruel* from the sky, forcing me to remove my near middle-aged corpse from the rock, my usual rock, and there are none here at the beach today- none but me and the gulls that screech, swirl and attack each other for things to eat that wash up, or float in.

A box of rain, it is, as I slip down the rock instead of clamber, scraping my back on sharp points and rested at the bottom, my shoes in sand, safe, pain, *my spine!* rain, and now a walk to the job-centre. "Sandy! You can kiss my little wet dick!" I say, *continuing*, as I exit the beach, my thoughts on how to kill Big Jim.

\*

*A box of rain will ease the pain and love will see you through*, sang The Grateful Dead, and I am jealous of their untimely death and curious about their words. Big Jim, is at the table, that same vest, his chubby, unshaven face involved with a fine lunch mother has prepared him, stood behind him, watching him eat, as if he was some kind of *special man*, my father. Watching him eat is akin to seeing pigs at the trough- he shovels in baked-beans laced with hot-dogs with a big old spoon; his other hand holds his pint, that washes the hot slop down with every gluttonous mouth-full frequently.

Why isn't he dead? I wonder, as mother, catches me wickedly eye-balling him, is jolted into action: "Do you want some, Clarence?

"No, I'm fine. Thanks," I tell her, secretly hungry, but choosing not to eat in spite of him, Big Jim. He's the real loser, I decide, unsure as he slops more glowing red sauce down his vest, knowing I'm still wearing three-to-four day old underpants and socks, yet aware of my hygiene issues since Sandy's departure, unlike him, aware of nothing since his departure from his rancid mother's womb.

*Oh, Sandy!*

We had a home together, in the City, a proper cat, plans of a family. She, a journalist, earning good money-

"To support your sorry ass!" she would tell me, hate-fully towards the end as I took drugs on the sofa listening to records, planning a best-selling novel, for years.

And, *Oh*, how the end broke me!

"Isn't it nice to have your father back home, Clarence?" mother, asks me, that hideous *spirited* tone she has when she is unsure; and, like me, she is unsure about practically everything.

"No," I respond, blank, a flicker of hatred, and Jim, notices, puts down his spoon.

"There's that *fag*-attitude again!" he moans, some beans on his chin. "Always gotta' spoil it! Miserable *e'* is, mother, *eh?*" he grins, slapping her on her big behind and she whelps and grins back at him. Finding his spoon, he says- "You'd better get *t'*job now too!" Pointing it at me, he continues- "W*u*rk-shy like *yoo* need *t'* git up off yer lazy asses! Mayor Scrimshaw, said!"

"Yeah, and Mayor Scrimshaw's a fat, lazy fuck like you!" I risk, getting up, finding the kitchen door quickly for fear of repercussion, those big, meaty fists, the bruising they leave.

"Come back here you lazy fag!" he shouts from the kitchen as I dart up the stairs and into the sanctity of my bedroom, locking the door behind me. "I've done me time! Tell *im'* mother! I've been d*oo*n mines long *e'*nuff, yer cunt!" he yells, as I collapse onto my bed, pulling my semen-stained black sheets around me and finding fetal-position, that really does help, I find.

*Why won't he die?* I wonder, as the tears begin to run.

\*

The ruin of Saggy Alice's stately home, rotting at a surprising rate, has become home to squatters, thieves, skaters, chavs and villains, since last year when she was found swinging and blue. It was on the very next morning that the mysterious, disgusting corpse of Morgwar, washed up on Sunny Beach, too.

Some say ancient, Blithe House, is cursed.

That night, next to a burning bin in the Grand Foyer, Skeleton-Bill, sat drinking and roasting a dead squirrel, with his dear old friend, Barnacle Bob, once a mariner, now a tramp. "There's an ill-wind blowin' off them thar oceans, there is!" said Bill.

"Aye!" said Bob. "It has been one year *t'* day they found the ol' girl swingin' upstairs!"

"Aye!"

"And the Morgwar!" grinned Bob, wickedly, turning his impaled squirrel in the fire, hairless, but for a bit of manky fur on the tail. They could have eaten better, but neither wanted to risk the town after the previous evening's drinking antics.

"Pis*h* and shite everywhere!" Constable Clemmancy, had told the Chief that very morning, totally fed up with Bill and Bob, *the toiletbowl men*, as they were known. "Dirty cunts!" he had complained. "I'm sick of em'! Drinking d*oo*n public lavvy again! Wait till' I git me hands on em' chief!"

"Make sure you wear gloves!" Chief Baker, had advised him, a usual seriousness, indignation.

*

"We're lucky they d*oo*nt come an arrest us, aft*a* last night, Bill, we *arr!*"

"Aye! Ere' *ava* bit *a* squirrel!" he offers, tearing a chunk of roasted flesh with his dirty, mitten-fingers.

"Ta!"

It was at that moment something shuffled, beyond the grand-arched, crumbling broken door-way, and both men went stiff, silent, Bill, his bit of squirrel-meat poised in his open, tooth-less mouth.

"What was that?"

Morgwar slithered into the temporarily moon-lit doorway.

The screams of the old sea-dogs were heard in town!

*

"Have you ever seen a squirrel jumping between branches?" Old Ned Skeletons, a distant relative, asks me, at the library. "They are *effortless* as they breeze between branches!"

"What's your point, Ned?" His beard is grey, matted; he

resembles the many old books he houses. From behind reading spectacles, he says, earnestly-

"You should jump branches! Get out of that damn house!"

"Can't afford it," I respond, coolly, honestly; "I've tried counting it up in my brain many times," I rant, "the cost of getting out, another place of my own. Not easy for the single, widowed, unemployed gentleman-actor-writer!"

"Well, I would suggest you could come and live with me, but as it is I've got a houseful!"

"Oh."

"Yes, cats and my dead wife's old friends! She was a traveller, part of her work, picked up many stray friends in her time; some of them, in their need, found their way here, to me!"

"Oh."

"They're nice people, from all over the world.."

"Are they illegal immigrants, Ned?" I ask him, suspecting foul-play.

"No, well, *yes*. They *may* be, but they keep me company and keep the place fairly tidy."

"Oh."

"Branch-out, like the squirrel!" he advises me, again, beaming-beard, handing my freshly-scanned pile of books to be borrowed by me, back to me. "*Ooo!* What's this?" he queries, as he finds a C.D of Figgy Shitdust's *The King*. "This takes me back!" he rambles, examining the cover, raising a bushy eyebrow, grinning at a very young Figgy, guitar, that puff of white hair, bolt of lightening, jump-suit and a Christmas-cracker pink, paper-crown on the top of his puff, a shit-eating grin, snout hanging from his bright purple lips and one hand giving a middle-finger.

"I've heard it's a real pooper!" I tell him.

"Yes, this is the one Shitdust, did before his classic.."

"I Hate Literally Everything?"

"Yes. It got very bad reviews, did, The King." He makes a

strange, guttural sound. "Poor, poor Figgy. Oh, well, that'll be 20p, please, Clarence. Oh, and, start playing the guitar again; that'll cheer you up, lad! But try not to play it like Figgy, did, *eh?* Here! You could be a busker?"

"What! In this town!" I tell him, slipping The King, into my lightweight black leather jacket, the books into a Right-Price carrier-bag, I had ready, and have unfolded, ready to receive the books for the distance home. "I would rather be dustbin-man than a busker in this place!"

"That's a good idea! Dustbin-man!" Ned calls out to me as I leave the library via the newly-installed sliding automatic doors.

\*

"Reality is not a flower," I muse to myself as I sit atop the milking-shed, alone, that night, David Webb on my mind, cool; a rare sense of peace, Amon Duul II on the phones. In the near-distance, the sound of the odd cow, as it finds nightmare, yet, I like the milking-shed. I have been coming here since child-hood, this very rooftop, where the stars twinkle brighter than down on the beach with cheap cider. It is here where the words come to me, from those many pipes downstairs here at the local creaming factory, and one thing you can say about Sunny Beach, is the quality of their fucking dairy!

\*

Track number 5 on Figgy's The King, skips annoyingly as I attempt to write a review on it.

*Track 5 – Shit On My Doorstep*, I write into my PC. A jangly mess of a tune, where Fig hounds us with three-chord riffs, as unpleasant to the ears as Kruegar's green and red sweater was to eyes years later. The drums sound like dust-bin-lids, and the song, like the previous 4 sound as if they have been recorded in an alley. A really dirty alley.

Nasty Fucking Studios, was where this mess of an album finds prog-attempt-in-garage-punk-metal-Frankenstein-conclusion, and finds really only a miserable whining queen of a drug and rape addict, in a bush, crying. This is a sorry final song, where legendary Sid Nasty, also Fig's best mate at the time, gets on the mic, backing-vocals- whines about vegetables, sea, custard and waiting for his then girlfriend, Suzy-Q, whom, like poor Backy Wackyblack, also failed in rehab. This certainly adds a little heart-felt angst to Doorstep, revealing a little of the lot of talent he actually had on Everything! His wild-success album to follow! What a man! I think as the C.D skips towards the end, as they all fucking do, with time. Tapes were better, I wonder, totally sick and bored of Shitdust. *His whining* in King, is as pathetic as mine, I shall write to the MGTOW community later- my real family I never see or hear from either as they have gone their own way.

Figgy Shitdust – The King -*1977/Nasty Fucking Records.*
1/5

\*

Chilly sits at his desk. "Tap dem shoes nihha'!" he says, pronouncing his g's, h's, as usual.

It is a weird dream, inspired by Black Stallion, a B-Movie rip off blaxploitation of Scarface, and better.

It is a dream.

And Courtney *love* is my girlfriend, and *he*, Chilly, I am. "Get dem niggas'! Got em!"

Even, Expert Reporter, Louis Threroux, throughout, is there, digging deep, dirty in my psycho-candy, sonic dream of marrying Thursday Yorke's bird- her bass, and girly dresses!

How I am in love with them all, drunk on cans! Those grungy

ones!

And King Curt, I am. As Dinosaur impersonate me, Saggy Alice, swinging from her chains, betters them.

*Slut, Kiss, Curl...*

Oh, she promised me...

Twelve cans and a nibble of Crunk, stolen from Big Jim.

*I have my records!*

And Pretty On The Inside, is a wonderful feminist response to King Curt- a kick in the balls back to the bent-back punker, whom, was lesser than Courtney, I shiver, Sliver, my little cock in my hands.

*But.*

As I consider, Alice In Chains, Dirt, I remember that it was the men who won the grunge war, no' the skanky, beautiful, beautiful women of grunge.

"Louis! You should have banged that whore!" I tell him, falling deeper into black butter and the warmth of Melvins.

\*

Suddenly my song is Slayer, and it paints my world blood, as usual.

*Morgwar!*

Focus!

And my little cock becomes massive, a big, shiny head, thick-stork!

Fuck those grungy cunters!

World Painted Blood, I scream!

\*

The very next morning, Big Jim, busted into my bedroom. Masturbating, I was, furiously; "Like a dog!" he screamed, throwing an empty can at me. "If ye wanna wank, do it w' dog, d*oo*nstairs!" he told me. "Jackin' off te' men, I'll bet! Fag!"

*

"Follow the yellow-fag road," Big Jim, chuckles, at luncheon downstairs that day. He flaps his bingo-wings. "Squawk! Squawk!" he does. "Yankin' te' men were ye!"

"Yeah, Jim," I tell him cool, as Lou Reed. "I was wanking to you, wanking to me. Chuckle on a dick! To Me To You! Now fuck off!" I tell him, exiting the kitchen as Elvis once exited buildings, doing the Fonz.

*

Pleased with myself I wander up the lonely cliff-trail. It winds higher, higher, occasionally allowing one a peek of the north sea; a sea that grows mightier, bigger the higher one gets. And as I get higher, deeper into that lonely trail, a blank sea-mist descends, suddenly, as they often do, and absorbed in a ghostly-white blanket of salty-silence I am. So thick it grows, that at certain moments I can see only my feet, the muddy, weedy trail to guide me up to the very craggy top.

The top, where the salty mist thins, and mother-ocean opens her arms to me, and blows a cool-wind at me, where I find the solitary bench, in memory of Captain Skag Skeletons 1866 - 1899, and I seat myself and allow the Sunny Cliffs spectacle to unfold.

It was at that very moment as I settled that I heard a strange, distant wail, a gargled *growl*- it drifted from beyond those jagged cliffs somewhere, right up to me, left me in an uneasy shiver, then trailed-off, out into the Big Beyond, The Other, The North Sea.

*Morgwar!*

He has come, some say- *It* has come back! And Bill and Bob,

The Toiletbowl Men, are still missing, after several late-night tramps and ravers reported hearing blood-soaked screams, not long after midnight, the other night!

*Morgwar!* Legendary Morgwar, who has haunted this Bay since records began. And Sunny Beach, is ancient- *once*, it was much larger, almost a City, some said, named Mathergarr, swallowed by the sea, now; out there in the mist that glowed eerie on certain nights, fisherman warned. When Mathergarr went down, *Morgwar, came up!* They say, in these parts, and have said for aeons.

*The Keeper!*

And once, every six years, *Morgwar comes!* Slithers back to shore and kills in sacrifice to Elder beings who once ruled here, they say!

This year, they found a disgusting corpse on the beach, something huge, unknown, dangerous looking with many sharp teeth and slippers. Some said it was Morgwar; I, am inclined to believe that it was only a baby!

\*

I find my pre-prepared, wrapped Wotzit sandwich in my pocket, munch on it, enjoy the cheese, the ocean, the fragrance and taste of cheese and ocean.

And then, I hear it again! That wail, *moan*, growl!

I get up, creep nearer to the cliff-edge, the wooden fence that protects suicidal ones, and granny-dumpers from doing so, *peer* over. "What was that?" I ask the cold, brisk wind, taking another bite of my sandwich, the uneasy feeling growing.

Leaning on the fence, I *peer* over, longer, best I can, imagine a tentacle suddenly grabbing me, pulling me over, never to be seen again, like Richie Manic of The Preachers! Yet, I don't think he died by sea-monster, and neither am I, today, as instead, the wind eases, the brown, cold ocean tumbles, stampedes of dirty white horses, down there, dissatisfied that I shall not die by sudden-tentacle as my last bit of Crunk, stolen from Jim, does its thing.

\*

On the way home, the afternoon finding darker cloud, rain, as always; the trail down was nerve-wracking! If only there had been a dog-walker, jogger or drug-dealer to take the sinister edge off of that lonely descent of a come-down. Often, I thought I saw a tentacle, was frightened, then excited, the disappointment as the tentacle turned out to be a curl of mist, or a twisting branch. And the hideous sound, I had heard, up there, I heard not again as made it back to the town from those dreaded cliffs, I did. Even as a child, that place had felt like a risky place to play, despite the obvious risks, and as they crumble slowly into the ocean, following ancient Mathergarr, its deadly keeper of her infinite secrets, *Morgwar, awaits!*

\*

I went to visit old-Ned Skeletons, the librarian, that evening. A little bare-chested Chinese fella in underpants told me he was out back, in his converted mobile library, where he lived, it seemed.
"You have a bed in here, Ned! You live out here!"
"Aye! I prefer it."
"Did the squatters kick you out, Ned?"
"Aye, I mean, *noo!* Like I say, I like it out here, in the old van! This was my father's you know! He did the rounds for years in this! It's a local treasure!"
I look around. There are still a few shelves around, carrying books, his dirty underpants and vests. There is a little table, and I remember colouring there while my mother chose books here as a

toddler. It is true, the old mobile-library is an institution, I consider, as I seat myself at that same little table, now, forty years later, this van, broken-down, rusting, rotting in Ned's back garden, the tall grass, his remnants of a sorry meal on a chipped plate, not fun-coloured crayons and pictures of clowns and ducks to colour, no, instead there is a squatter's clutter! "You own this property, Ned! Boot em' out! Move back into your own house!"

"Aye!" he grins, and I wonder about Ned's conviction to living a normal life ever again. *If he's happy here, he's happy!* I conclude, as the kettle on the camping-stove boils, whistles and exudes steam. *He may be bullied?* I ponder, knowing about that. He fixes us tea, and continues to present me with random books I may be interested in.

"Got any books on Morgwar?" I ask him eventually, his enthusiasm for books insatiable.

"Morgwar!" he beams, stroking his beard. "Aye! I got a book on Morgwar!" he cackles, getting up to scan a shelf. "This is the best Morgwar book out there," he rambles, finding it. "Very rare! You can borrow it," he tells me, handing me the dusty, old, slim-tome, "but, I must have it back!"

"Poems Dedicated To The Sea," I say, reading the title. And on the front, a hideous picture of Mighty Morgwar, himself! Long, sharp teeth, gills, flippers, tentacles and black flubber!

*And those eyes!*

Beady, black pin-pricks of danger, many of them, evil. "That is a shockingly-real picture!" I tell Ned, shuddering. In Morgwar's claw there is a mermaid, and he has crushed her like toothpaste over the beach. His claw-feet stand in a puddle of her.

"Aye!" he said, "and Do Not read these poems aloud, on *t'*beach at night!" he warns me, wide-eyed, a sudden change in him, for the worse. "For it is said that if they are spoken aloud, they will summon the mighty beast himself from ruined undersea Mathergarr, and kill us all!"

*

Two hours later I was on the beach reciting weird poems to the wind: "Mathergarr, *Mighty Mathergarr!*" I yelled, holding torch-light to the book. "City Of *More* And Much! Such secrets you take with you to these brown oceans, leaving behind but a corner of you! Sunny Beach, they have called it, covering your black-secrets, mighty Mathergarr, yet, within these words holds the power to bring back The Keeper! For *he* has been to Mars! And cry from these pages, a call, to rile thine Mighty Keeper, of slime and *teeth!* Morgwar!" I scream. "*Mighty Morgwar!*"

There is a flash of lightening and I duck for cover as another hits the beach in sparks. Thunder rumbles, an ominous omen, and I wonder about my antics here tonight! *But you must see it through*, the Devil inside me whispers with a tenderness I can not deny, as I have often, the devil.

I find the page, carry on...

*

Big Jim was at the kitchen table, finishing the last of his whiskey bottle. "Where's that f*oo*kin' lad o' mine?" he asks aloud, banging his fist as the thunder bangs outside, rain lashing at the window. Mother, sat also at the table doing a crossword puzzle in the daily gazette, stopped to look up at him.

"You know he's forty-two now, Jim?" she says. "Maybe you should lay o*of* him a bit?"

"F*oo*k im!" says Jim, firing an Eagle. He offers mother the pack, she accepts, chain-smoking, as always, especially in the evening. "It's nearly 12! What's e' doin'? *E'*s still got te' answer f*ur* way e' spoke *t'* me earlier, the black fag!"

Suddenly, Clarence Nutkins Skeletons, burst in, pale as a ghost, out of the storm.

"Where the f*oo*kin' ell' a' y*uu* b*i*n?" Jim shouted.

"Up your fat arse!" his grown son shouted back, a dim-red, very menacing glow in Clarence's eyes that prevented his old man from getting up from the table, this time as he swept past both his parents like a demonic shadow, sweeping up the stairs where the door slammed shut.

"I wonder what's got in't' him?" said mother, timid.

"*Dick!* That's what!" said father, stubbing out his cigarette and getting up to let in their pet dog, Butch, who had followed Clarence home from the storm, it seemed, as he scratched, whined at the door. "Get in shit-legs!" Jim told Butch, wrestling with the door as the winds raged. "Wha' *t'* fkin' night!" he moaned, his final words before two big slimy claws dragged him screaming into the night, mother left stunned and Butch whimpering in the corner. His terrible screams as he was torn apart were heard even as the unholy tempest raged, and upstairs, a different Clarence, glowing red eyes sat silently, knowing of the terrible carnage that was about to ensue, all over town, and Big Jim, or Daddio, was no more, for sure.

# THREE

60

"Rabbit, Rabbit, Rabbit.." says Chav.
"Rabbit, rabbit, rabbit.." says Dave.
"Rabbit, rabbit," threatens Chav.
Raising his old hairy, gold-ringed fists, South-Paw, Dave said- "Go on, cunt! Say it one time!"
"Rabbit!" said Chav.
And the meat-pumps reigned.

\*

Later, in the pub, Chav, suggested to Dave, that rather than taunting each other, they should get a new piano, despite their old age and start writing songs again, a new Christmas Album. "Think of it Dave! A new Joanna! One last crack!"

"I like it Chav! A new Joanna anna' Christmas Album. And a farewell three-day piss-up on the end of Great-Yarmouth pier, me ol' mucker! Have it!"

*

"Old Mrs Brown's dirty knickers!" sang Chav, hammering brand new piano keys, practising their new song, Old Mrs Brown's Dirty Knickers!

Dave was on his new banjo, eager as a ration-book-window-cleaner, leg-a'-tapping, pint on. "Shitty old brown dirty knickers! She has!" pumps-up, Dave, pinching his nostrils, doing a face, practising his gag for the video, loving it.

"She hangs her washing in the morning!"

"Her titties in the evening!"

Suddenly- "Oi!" someone screams. "Turn it in would ye! We're next door working with violins! We don't need this racket!"

"Fuck off!" Chav, gives him. "All the line is taken," he sings, his arms and hands springing back to life on the new Joanna.

"And mothers fryin' bacon!" gives it Dave, his frisky banjo!

And together- "And Mrs Brown is drying out her dirty drawers!" They finish.

"Jesus giddy fucking wept," uttered the visitor.

# FOUR

"Jingle Bells, Jingle Bells, mother-fuckers!" says old, Chinese Roy, looking around for the hiding teddy slaves. "Come on out, you little bitches! Papa's got a gift!"

"We won't come, Roy!" says Fingers, from a darkened shadow in the black corner of the office. "You tried to fuck Rosy! Pervert!"

"Yes, *Fingers!* And when I get hold of you, I'm going to put my long fingers inside you, *Fingers*, and rip you apart! I want to know which of you little bastards wrote that letter to Veronica! And I also want you to know that the penis-flesh-pie, is a very good idea, so I may not kill you," says Roy.

"You can't kill us, Roy!" says Captain Dimples. "We're Voodoo Teddys, from Space! You're fucked mate!"

"As for you, *Dimples*, a microwave awaits!" Roy tells him as Ted The Terrible scuttles past his legs. "Come here! I see you!"

And then- "BASTARD!" he screams as he realises Ted, has put knife to leg again, slicing through his Ghi. "That's it! Death!" and clutching his wound he limps to his desk, fumbling at a drawer. The Teddys chuckle in the shadows, enjoying the anger of Roy, as he retrieves a handgun.

Suddenly, there is a crackle on the intercom; Roy's driver, Bert, or *Berty*, as Roy called him -temporarily filling in duties as PA, as Veronica, is still *gone* to the north of the City, bigger, better things, she told everyone- says: "The police are here, sir!"

"Fuck!" responds Roy, gun in claw, leg bleeding.

*

"Mr Chiao, we've received an angry complaint about a letter, supposedly sent by you, to a Miss *Veronica Cartwright..*"

"I can explain.."

"Can I come in?"

"If you must, Officer. Berty will show you the way down."

*

Seated at Roy's large desk, Officer Smith, looked around him.
Roy's Weird Arts Ltd.
LAS Alberto!
A pitch-black painted, winding brick dungeon that reeked of heady incense all the time. Some minimalist nasties as you descend the steep, old brick steps deeper into the building, where at its deepest point is an extensive subterranean Art Gallery. "This is an interesting place you have here, Mr Chiao!" Says Smith, dropping his grim wonder to look at his dirty notes, the sound of a tube-train passing somewhere nearby. "Are you OK, sir? You seem.."

"Tired? *Yes!* Very tired, Officer! Am planning a new exhibition and it is *wery* demanding."

"Oh. What's the new exhibition?"

"Penis."

"Penis?"

"Oh, yes," Roy, giggles gingerly, reaching inadvertently for his wounded leg, stinging from the cut, still leaking blood, despite the dish-cloth he wrapped tightly around it in haste. "That is the name and theme of our new exhibition, starting in February."

"Oh. So, tell me about this letter Miss Cartwright, received the other day."

Roy, takes a deep breath, still boiling with anger at the still-hiding teddys, a twisted Christmas present, responsible effectively for this unwanted intrusion of The Law, and still reeling from the loss of Veronica, his assistant -*love*- of many years; gone right before Christmas, to his sworn enemy, Gator-Sinbad-Tool. "I... I didn't write it!" he declares.

"Who did, Mr Chiao?"

"Enemies!" says Roy, his long eyebrows, goatee and helmet-long-hair, black, all perched on a purple shiny Ghi, ferreting in it for his pack of cigarettes. "I have many enemies! Many art-*haters* and racists around here, there are! Ignorant people everywhere!"

"It is a rather disturbing letter, Mr Chiao! Death-threats, vile insults etc; Do you know specifically who wrote this and why?"

"Yes and no."

"Yes and no?"

"Would you like some tea, Officer Smith?"

"No. So, it wasn't you who wrote the letter, Mr Chiao?"

"No!"

"I see."

\*

"Kevin, Jackal! You have to get rid of them! I was nearly

arrested over a letter one of them wrote! I had the police, here!"

"Teddys can't write letters!" says Kevin Valentine, Roy's number one Artist; a chubby, middle-aged scruffy little man with a few days worth of wiry beard, patches of hair that still grew on his round, bald head, growing, a Right-Price jogging-suit, trainers, glowing yet soiled, in-fact, Cornelius, as he sometimes pretentiously called himself, looked more like a painter-decorator, than an artist. A drunk, cowboy one, you see often on The Watchdog, on tele.

"Don't be so sure!" says Jack Jackal, double the size of both of the others; He resembles The Undertaker, from WWE, but a more unhealthy, shit-kicker version, his gnarled cowboy hat and pitch-black eyes, enormous muscles going slowly to flab. "I've seen those teddys do things you wouldn't believe!" he says, fiddling with one of Roy's many wind-up toys he has on his desk today. He winds up the teeth, lets them clack across the surface. "Where are they, anyway?"

"Fuck knows!" says Roy, watching the gnashing-teeth with feet hop, then slowly run out of juice, and stop. In his long claw, he has a monkey with cymbals, ready-wound, and he lets it go, on the trail of the teeth. "They come and go! But this time they've been gone for nearly two days, hiding. And why you call them *Teddy Slaves?* They do nothing to help!"

"They gave you the penis-flesh-pie idea?" offers Kevin, eyeballing Jack, concerned about handing ownership of the Voodoo Teddys to another maniac, and cannibal-pies.

"I would have figured that idea out on my own, given enough time!" whines Roy, waving his claw as the little monkey stops banging and grinds to a halt next to the teeth.

"And, they were nice to you when you first let them out of their box! *Right*, Jack?"

"Yeah! So, you see, Roy- the teddys helped you out! Sped-up the big dick idea!" grins Jack, picking up the grinning monkey to examine it.

"Come to think of it- how are you going to get *penis-flesh*, Roy?" asks Kevin, querulously. "And more importantly, are you serious about serving penis-pie to guests on the opening night?"

The black office goes suddenly cold, *blacker*, dimmer and somehow hostile, despite the many winding, soothing, sweet-smelling smoke-ripples of incense sticks, dotted around. "I'm deadly serious... and I know a man," says Roy, that familiar Devil's twinkle about him, teasing a petal of his bone-white Orchid flower with a delicate claw.

"I wanna' see that letter to Veronica!" announces Jack, getting up to prowl around Roy's office, the top of his hat brushing the top of the grimy-brick ceiling as he does so.

"No. You don't!"

"Yes, I really do! Why don't you have your office upstairs, *Roy?* It's dingy as fuck down here!"

"I don't need windows, Bigfoot!" says Roy, lighting a cigarette in his elegant holder, waving another claw. "I don't want to see the city all day long; *Distressing!* I like the dark, the damp..."

"The rats?"

"Yes. I like them too. The creatures of the underworlde are my friends."

Another tube-train rumbles by, nearby.

"So, *Penis*, it is. February?" questions Kevin.

"Yes!" beams Roy.

"I think a *wee* celebration is called for!" announces Jack, having returned to his seat after stretching his tree-trunk legs. "Buzz through to ol' Berty! Tell him to get the drinks and drugs out on a nice silver tray!"

"Good idea!" signals Roy, cracking his long fingers then allowing a long-index to reach a big red button. "Berty!"

"Sir?"

"Drinks, drugs, chicken-crisps, egg-roll and PK nuts, to the office, now, my good man!"

"Yes, sir."

"And if you see just one of those furry little bastards, send them down here, immediately! Or try to stamp on it!"

"Yes, Mr Chiao."

*

That night in his sleeping-quarters, Roy, donned his sleeping cap and snuffed the black candles. Still half-cut, semi-crunked, he pulled the duvet over himself, snuggled into the rippling, heated waterbed and stared into the spinning, mysterious dark. "Where the hell are they?" he wondered, caressing himself, as usual, concerned at the continued absence of his *teddys*, glad, yet sad somehow that they may have jumped-ship, like Veronica, his dear Veronica. "Yes! *That's it!*" he barked, before falling asleep, the distant sounds of Old London, around him outside in his *Playground*, as he often called the City. "They've gone to Gator! Like precious, Veronica..." he uttered, *faded*, and almost a tear.

*

He was awoken by a loud banging on his bedroom door. *Bang! Bang! Bang!* "For fuck's sake!" he complained, rubbing eyes, lighting a candle, checking the time on his precious Daffy-Duck bedside alarm-clock. Daffy, was Roy's fav character of the Looney's. "Who's there?" he called out.

Silence.

3AM.

"Who's there?" he called out, again, removing himself from his waterbed, finding slippers, cane, his purple dressing gown with the golden capital letters ROY, embroidered on the back of it.

Silence.

And then, he remembered- *the teddys!* "I know it's you," he said, creeping to the door. "Berty never *bangs* my door.." and he paused, suddenly, the wild, hopeful idea that it might be Veronica -tall, dark, beautiful Veronica- behind his bedroom door, come home finally. "But at this hour?" he whispered, pined, feeling the pain of her loss again, knowing she was probably tucked-up with big Gator Tool, the rich, posh north-side of the city, a posh four-poster, a massive mansion. "It can not be her!" he concluded, finding the door-handle, angry now, ready to swing it open and take-on the intruder.

He did.

Outside, in the freezing, silent corridor, the flickering light from Roy's candle, rattling on the candlestick-holder, he saw, in his uneasy mix of angriness, apprehension, a scrap of paper on the floor with thick crayon scribbles on it. He picked it up, read it-

*Roy.*

*We want to play a game with you.*
*If you can catch us, we will be your slaves.*
*If we catch you, YOU will be our slave!*

*Love.*
*Teddys xx*

\*

"Bastards!" shouts Roy, at the breakfast table. Berty is at the stove, fixing his master a boiled egg, soldiers, the windowless kitchen steamy, damp, cold. "Oh, and make them slim, *hard* soldiers today! I'm going to war!"

"I beg your pardon, sir?"

"War!" he declares, his beady eyes scanning The Bumblebee Gazette for morning news of interest. "3AM! Berty! *3AM!* One of those little bastards left me that note! They want to play games? I'll show them *toys* how to play games! And, be sure to remind me to telephone Jack and Kevin, later; let them know that their Christmas Presents have re-appeared!"

"How's that leg, sir?" enquires stony Berty, buttering the little soldiers, his little frilly-apron, that was once Veronica's, over his old, dusty grey suit using a butter-knife, Roy, bought with him from Asia, once his mother's, he told Berty- "Dead mothers! Thank God!" he had said.

"It's healing, slowly. *Bastards!* I shall still need to be re-bandaged, also, today! *Ah!* Egg!" says Roy, receiving one, happier suddenly. He loved egg.

*

Roy, Jack and Kevin, loiter that afternoon downstairs in The Gallery Of Horrors, as some call it. They stand next to Kevin's masterpiece, Golden Bigfoot, all three staring at it; a somehow serene piece, despite the subject matter. "The penis-flesh-guy, Roy?" enquires Jack, a glass of Champagne in his meaty-maw, those fingerless, studded-leather-gloves, highly inappropriate for such a slender vessel. "It wouldn't happen to be *Joe Don Baker*, by any chance, would it?"

Roy, grins, a sleazy gash he is known and feared for- "Joe Don, is indeed a valuable contact, who has many contacts, and that is all I shall say!" He puts a long finger to his lips, indicating quiet, and Kevin, shudders inadvertently.

"Fair enough!" barks Jack; "*Now*, let's have a look at that note."

Roy, losing his smirk, reaches into his Ghi-pocket, pulls out the sinister scrap of paper that was left last night at his bedroom door, hands it to Jack.

"*Yeah!* That's teddy handwriting!" says Jack, passing it to Kevin, who has also suffered badly before in the past due to The Teddy Slaves, yet strangely brightened to see that familiar writing.

"*Yep!* That's them!" says Kevin. "I used to get notes like this. They play games and punish you, if they sense you are not cooperating!"

"So, what are you going to do about it, Roy?" asks Jack.

Grinning again, Roy, sups some of his bubbly, says - "I'm going to play *their* game! That is what I am going to do. I'm going to win, and then, I'm going to kill them all!"

"*Cheers!*" announces Jack, and the three men chink their glasses in salut.

There are a few people in the gallery, milling about, yet, none seemed interested in the three strange men, or, those guests were just simply scared of them.

"To the hunt!" says Kevin.

"To the game!" says Jack.

"To the death!" says Roy.

\*

Cargo Ship – Brown Sugar
Star-date 2044 – Earth Time
Destination- Mars
Condition – Green
Cargo – Rice, Food grain, seeds, grass.

Captain Chiao, slicked his moustache. On the monitor, Burt Reynolds, the actor, fights thugs. "Go on!" says the Captain, slinging more SKY down his neck, his boots up on his station. "That's it!" he cheers, mimicking a few punches as Burt, mops-up on-screen. "Those were the days!" reminisces the ageing skipper, sloshing around what is left in his bottle, before sinking it. "Well, I'm drunk enough," he tells himself, as maintenance men, Chiles and Ray, enter the leisure-quarters via sliding doors. "Smokey and The Bandit! You all done?"

"Yes, sir!" says Chiles, removing his gloves, a look on his black face, blacker with oil and grime that suggests *really* done.

"It's done," says Ray, his assistant, a fat man with long hair and a mangey beard.

"And so are we, captain!" reiterates Chiles. "Shit, man! You drank all that whiskey by yourself?"

"Yeah, I'm shitfaced! And Japenese whiskey is like fine, fine wine! I thought you two would have been finished hours ago!"

"So did we!"

Suddenly, a terrific explosion; instant fire, *shrieking...*

\*

Roy, woke with a start, screaming- "Cosmia Gallactic! Cosmia-Gallactic!" He would have sat upright, had he not been tied down. "*Wha..* what is this?" he said, desperate, wriggling, struggling to move, but he was bound, with many ropes across him, locking him tight to his bed in the gloom.

And then, he remembered, and- "MOTHER FUCK!" he screamed, as unseen Voodoo teddys began to giggle in the black.

## FIVE

Something very strange, almost hip happened to Joe Giblet, when one day he discovered Gluey Porch Treatments, by a mysterious, ugly band called The Melvins, by God.

\*

At the job-centre, I ponder, very drunk, one digit per key here, high, how like Aragon, from the rings, I am, fucking wasted in fact, bongos going, dead irks.

And liv Tyler, my wide-mouth love of elvish sensuality, I have never recovered- her big, perfect red lips. Aragon, he, the dream.

Now the dreamer.

Fiercer.

Her snow white dwarf face-

I kissed, my hand around my dick wondering of the wizardry, the real cinematic wizardry of Peter Jackson, as Richard Branston,

mocks me with his company of amazing witches.
My God!
Heaven.
*Thou have passed!*

\*

*And then there was the very odd Radio-head, his creep, and words, few, that came with an eye. And I wept, explaining to his dream that I was sick of putting things that are now considered hip into my own work. And he told me to shut the fuck up.*

\*

*Happy trails..*
*Happy trails..*
I am in the grass, down the Green, cider done hours ago, a little sleep next to a dog-shit, I notice, the last four hours or so- The sun's going in, and few are about as I struggle to get up. God I feel like shit, I notice, pulling me jacket tight as the drizzle sets in, a freezing mist creeps across the green, to Paradise Estate, where I live, among junkies, blacks and all that. It's a right shit-hole, that is true, I consider, as I eye it over the green, her many arms, fingers and towers- and mine, some lights on in there this evening, where the little class A-hobbits scuttle by day and howl and shriek at night!

I've lived here all me life, Paradise Estate, Las Alberto! Old-London, so many names, so many wonders. The record store I owned once, better days, was named, So Many Wonders, until, in the 70's, I changed it to, Better Days, then in the 90's, Gone To The Digital Dogs, a title of wit and humour, I was proud of, for a while, until I went bankrupt.

And lost my wife.

And my cat.

And my daughter, who never calls, or visits, and that does hurt, and that is why I drink cider, and red wine, daily, to keep all those demons at bay, and the pain, away.

*

In the lift I see Albert, a strange old man, who gives me the eyeball, as if to say- drunk again! And I nod him and tap for the 12$^{th}$. The doors come together, grey as prison doors as cock-length finds balls. Creative! I consider, as usual, always enjoying the cock and balls.

*Bing!*
*Bing!*

And here we are, the dreaded 12$^{th}$, where once I lived with my Granddad, until he died, twenty long years ago. "Oh! 20P!" I say, finding one in a puddle next to a butt-end, pocketing-it, happy of the coincidence, and certain that Mad Mike, as me other not-puffy Granddad, was known, still haunted this floor and rock-solid. "Bless his heart!" I say, doing the cross, then finding the door down a corridor of utter filth, remembering how as a child, Mad Mike would leave puddles of his victim's blood and teeth here, when the drug-deals etc, didn't work out.

*

I chuck a Deep-Pan into the beeper. She hums and bakes it good with a cheerful bing! I slip into the lounge, remove me denim, admire me Maiden patches, slump into the sofa and kick me boots.

"What a feelin'!" I say, flicking on the tele, finding the cartoon channel, burning me mouth with an impatient bite of me Chicago-Meat-Heat, smothered in extra olive-oil for the fuck of it, loving time away from the band, the boys, Sal. Me head's still banging from this afternoon's cider-on-the-lawn, but a dose of Spiderman, the old one, fine red-wine and feet-up'll cure the price.

And that was when it hit me, like a bill from SKYY-TV, always fucking heavy as I remembered that this evening would be different to the usual, lazy, lovely ones, stuffing me face, as Gay Old Greg, me Uncle, was coming over for cocktails, the posh cunt, I thought, banging me fist, knowing how hard it is to please gay-old-Gregoire, his thirst for conversation and bullshit. "Oh my fuck!" I whine, a huge cheese-web formed between my slice and gob. "Dirty old Greg and his double-kiss," I say, mouth-full of greasy-hot-peperoni.

*To be continued...*

    I thought, then he arrived.
    "Can I take your coat, Greg?"
    "No, it's mine!"
    "Ha! Would you like a drink?"
    "Hang on! You look like shit!"
    "Do I?"
    "Yes. And this place! What's happened? How's the band?" he giggles, oddly, revealing a gold tooth. He is very black, in black, in the black of my condo. "*Well?*" he beams, and I feel nervous.
    "It's nice to see you, Greg."
    "*Is it?* It smells!"
    "You smell nice, what cologne is that?"
    "A very expensive one! How long have you had the beard? There's cheese in it, and other things! God!" he recoils, revealing fine red wine, he has brought, and that takes the sting out of all of

this. "Where's the kitchen?" he muses, finding it himself.
 I follow him.
 "Spiderman!" he says.
 "Eh?"
 "On the TV!"
 "Oh. Yeah."
 "Do you have a bottle opener? Oh my god! It's worse in here than in there!" he laughs, really loud, and one of the neighbours yells-
 "Shut the fuck up!"
 "Jesus!" he says normally, winding cork.

## SIX

Christmas came early to White Lakes, that year, and so did death. Death came to visit in the snow-storm that left the whole area white, overnight, frozen in time, stranded, and the local Emergency Services struggled as the odd deaths began. Reports of people freezing-over, worried people told the Police, before the lines went dead.

*

Sidney Melville, watched from his bedroom window the snowflakes fall. He was a snowflake, too, his drunken father, *Pete*, had told him, once or twice and that bothered him; bothered him like Banshee screams, dead babies, dragon-ghosts, wizards in black.

The White Witch.

And his family were out of town visiting Grandfather Norman, who was ill. And Sidney, was ill; he had a broken leg- told his parents firmly he didn't fancy the trip, the annual boredom, old pops getting drunk with the younger one, a scream-up with mother, tuna sandwich then an hour or two in the car, those winding, curling roads that ran around the lakes, and left one feeling sick, dizzy. Margaret and little-Norm, his brother and sister could enjoy all that this weekend, without Sid; and he wasn't missing them, until now, maybe, as the silence set-in with the unexpected snow outside.

And the telephone wasn't working!

Would they be able to get back? On those roads! He doubted it; the few cars that had attempted to make it down the lane, out front, were now snowed-over; their owners just left them as the overnight blizzard worsened.

And now it was very silent.

Very silent indeed.

So silent, in-fact, that when a random wind moaned, he took it for a ghost, and huddled now, back on his bed, he wondered how long it would be before the babysitter arrived.

Janice!

Fat Janice would be here soon, he thought to himself, feeling better, pulling the blanket his grandmother knitted close around him, to keep him warm in a house that was getting colder by the hour. On his feet were two pairs of socks, his legs bore two sets of jogging bottoms, a big bandage. Two jumpers and a blanket, and still he found himself shivering, on occasion needing to get up, limp around the house with his crutches, like *Little Timmy Cratchett*, so Pete, said to him, going from room to room, peering from the frozen glass of the windows out into the storm-white outside that seemed to be showing no signs of stopping. It was as if the world had changed, overnight; and though beautiful, it was also deadly.

Next week it would be Christmas Day! He wondered, wondering how any of that was going to work out now.

Damn!

If only he could get the telephone to work! And his leg was starting to ache again as the afternoon was becoming evening. He couldn't have risked a walk into town, not in his condition, the weather outside, despite the noise of the sirens on and off all day.

What the hell was going on? Sid wondered, finding his claw-feet slippers and putting them on his hands to mimic a tiger.

Bang!

It came from downstairs, and like a tiger, Sid, went still.

"Sidney!" It was Janice.

He sighed. Thank God! "Up here!" he called.

"Can you come down?" There was trouble in her voice.

\*

"No-one really knows what is happening, Sid, but there's been some deaths!"

Sidney, froze. "Not..."

"No, not mum or dad!" said Fat Janice, cramming a doughnut into her rosy face, crumbs spilling. "Don't worry!"

"No. I meant Marge, and Norm!"

"Oh! Well, I'm sure they're OK. They'll be home tomorrow as planned, I'm sure!"

"Are you still staying tonight, Janice?"

"Yes! Of course! Now, come on, we need to get some candles on before nightfall. And make sure all the doors and windows are locked."

Sidney, sensed that Janice, wasn't telling him everything, and she was eating faster than usual, indicating worry, and Sid, worried about that too.

\*

Later on that evening, the storm as bad outside as it had been during the day, Sid and Janice, sat close next to the fireplace where a fire crackled pleasingly, heckled occasionally by fierce gusts that made it somehow back down the chimney, the odd hiss or sizzle as a snowflake made it down there too. Dotted around the living room were as many candles as they could find, which weren't as many as they would have liked, but it would do.

There was menace in the air.

"Do you believe in ghosts?" Sid, asked Janice.

"No! Of course not!"

She did.

"I think White Lakes is haunted!"

"That's ridiculous!"

"No, really! Ever since we found that baby in the river!"

"Let's not think about that! It's a shame the tele isn't working! Big Rising Stars is on with Simon Scowl! I love that! That, and biscuits, and doughnuts." Janice patted her big belly, fat with cake. Even she was feeling off tonight, scared, even, if she was honest.

"What board games do you have?" she asked him, spiritedly.

"Ghost Castle," he said, blank. "It's the only one. That or snap."

"*Snap!*" she said, getting up to visit the fridge that was slowly thawing. "And put another log on the fire! We'll sleep down here tonight, it'll be warmer," *and safer*, she thought, finding the butter dish, allowing herself a finger-scoop of butter that she sucked. Cracking a can of Coke, guzzling, belching a bit, she rifled deeper into the fridge. "Caramac!" she clapped, finding three bars and snatching them with her chubby fingers. "Would you like a Caramac, Sidney?" she called.

Silence.

A crackling fire in the room down the corridor.

Candles flickered in the kitchen, and her fat shadow wobbled like Mr Blobby.

A hideous moan.

Her blotchy skin prickled.

"Sidney?" she whimpered, before it came into the room and she froze, died, and collapsed, wide-eyed, Caramac in hand and shit down her fat legs.

## SE7EN

Mrs Ozzy Osbourne, the other side of the world felt it too, being a right old witch. She shook poor, tired Ozzy, who turned, moaned-

"Wha?" he groaned, those glasses on, suggesting to Mrs Ozzy, that he was back on the sauce again, despite his health!

"I don't know," she cackled, feeling cold, yet excited, her wide lips red and silly dog snuggled up.

"Get *t'*sleep woman!" moaned Oz, going back into his perfect dream. As usual, he was right, and Mrs Ozzy went right back off to sleep, cuddling her wiry poodle.

*

In McDonald's, someone who looks suspiciously like he may be the Ham-Burglar, waits in the massive queue.

I am out of my mind.

Big Mac.

And someone questioned me about Harry Potter, earlier.

Do you like it? I was asked.

Not really. I prefer The Worst Witch, n' Terrible Terry P, Ol' JK copied, sold, mansions later.

*In-fact,*

I said, rather firmly, but with kindness as to avoid law-suits and drama, as these types bring for shits and giggles, and politics.

JK can Potter-Off for all I care, I said, and rot in one of her many mansions, scratching her magic-muff, a traitor to real witches and wizards, as she fumbles at the keys for something original that she hasn't copied, that can buy another mansion for the immigrants, to mock them on the TV, she loves.

That is what I said.

*

I also complained to Satan, that day, about Jimmy Saville, Rolf, the boys! "Jesus!" I told him. "Couldn't you limit ye little demons to just one or two kiddies, ye nutta?"

He gave me a sorry, baby-face, his sad old horns.

"Oh! Don't feel bad! They're at an end, old chap! Come on! Horns-up! Let's roast another mall-rat!" I gave him, tickling his chin.

I love Satan.

Hail Satan!

\*

I have just spent my entire life in forced, self-imposed loser-hell/heaven- three years in solitude, recently, squalor, ranting into a keyboard for hours, unto nights. I pushed it further than fly-boy Kerouac, and took mountains of dope and buckets of ale and whiskey on the trip, matching, I reason, Hunter, himself, God Rest Him, Satan wake him.

And like lazy Buddha, feed him, I had no sex or pleasure-

And more than him, no cake.

Like Infinite Waters, the shaker to my salt, I tried no wanking and failed after day three.

And now,

I deserve a film made by Quentin Tarantino.

His eponymous last, for me, I have decided.

\*

8

Bobby Mallow watched the massive Saquatch and odd, pink Camel, struggling on two legs, humping things from their crashed spaceship, now a smoking wreckage in the trees, near the beach where The Marshmallows lived, in the little bit of marshes between forest and beach, the big puddles, their lakes, etc, and their little township was called Marshmallow Town, it was. "What a couple of fucking idiots," laughed Bobby, turning his mallow-flesh, pink, and he lit one, another ciggy, his first of the day. His girlfriend, Sallow Mellow, would moan, he knew, but he didn't worry about that, as he -allowing billowing smoke into the air- puffed away. In the background, Marshmallow Town, the morning fires as The Mello-Fellow made their eggs, bacon and liver. "Look at these two jokers!" continued Bob. "Like a very strange, psychedelic animal version of Laurel And Hardy!" he chortled, coughing a little blood-cream. "Shit!" he said, knowing that he should puff less, Doctor Puff, had told him, in a huff and stuff, and Bob, wondered if he would be able to give up the cigs? "Maybe I'll give up cigs if Sallow gives up Heroin?" he wondered, in a darkly serious moment, as the giant animals struggled, argued.

Hi! Ho! Silver!

That was the name of their spaceship, and Bob, wondered what treasures they may be able to scavenge from the smouldering wreck, flames still licking her insides greedily, suggesting it may be a very burnt haul. But a spaceship was rare on the island until

Dr Cleaves and his sinister Area 69, started-up, 169 days ago, many strange ships had landed, yes. Yet, none had crashed, or none that little Marshmallow Bobby, knew of, anyway.

*

*Something crashed. I open my eyes, reach for this notebook, in another dream, start to scribble- another strange, vivid dream tumbles away with the rest of the sleep I need. And the dream is gone, in dream.*

*Insomnia.*

*It was something I struggled with before Morgwar, before that dreadful night I have still to recollect fully. One year on, and those recollections, madnesses still elude me; and I sometimes think it's for the best.*

*Everyone's gone, everyone's dead. Well, not quite everybody, but that terrible night, one year ago, almost to the day, certainly cleansed Sunny Beach, almost destroyed it, I foretell- more mysteries surround that cataclysmic event than may or may not happen than ever before; Authorities, Scientists, from all over the world have converged here over the last year hoping to explain what exactly went down possibly that terrible night.*

*Down its throat!*
*And today.*
*I just don't know.*

*

*My name is Clarence N Skeletons. I am one of the survivors of the ordeal.*

*I am forty-five years old.*

*My remaining family are dead- my parents. My mother's brother reached-out, after the incident, and I refused his help, as I shall smug cousin, Dave. Something changed me on that strange night, and I have decided to stay quiet about it, for fear of being labelled mad and bundled away with other survivors to the institution in Brainchester; And many went mad that night! Stark raving insane, some of them as the monster...*

*I pause.*

*Breathe, attempt to clear my thoughts, visions, that indescribable feeling of dread that has lasted with me since that night. Often, in the long hours, in my room, the local authorities gave me, after our home was practically destroyed...*

*I pause.*

*Breathe.*

*Collapse.*

*They found me, so I am told, in that house, one side having collapsed completely, and me, in the other, my room, they told me, upstairs, sitting quietly, a vacant look, nothing to say, they said as Nuclear bombs went off and the world began to die. Shock, one Doctor told me. Normal, she told me. Normal, another told me;*

*She would become a ghoul.*

*And though I remember very little of that tempestuous night of mega-carnage, that terrible feeling remains.*

*Unanswered questions.*

*Death.*

*Death?*

*But I am still alive! How is this so, when so many others are so dead?*

*

*"It is well known that the French sell us only the dregs, the piss of their legendary wine," I whine, the dreaded ocean, a past that once was, could be again, should reality regain sanity. After what happened on that eponymous, blood-soaked night, I am unsure, yet certain now, a blood-red sky going down, my eyes going slowly yellow as the ghouls begin to scream from the ruins of Sunny Beach, red wine, a dirty bottle. My machete is sharpened, ready for the night, should any of them get too near my hideout- they will pay! Rivers of blood! And like Baby-cart, I am ready to go body-shopping!*

*

*"Oh Mad Wolf," I tell the blood sky, and she answers me back with the blackest of nights as I descend from my tower, the old lighthouse, where Ned Skeletons once watched the midnight oceans of the freezing north on darkest nights, narrow-weed eyes. "Such a moon!" I tell her, as she reveals herself on this, the beginning of my end. Forty-Four, or something, smoking, drinking away in another mad dream- and it does not matter.*

*I paint on my camouflage warpaint, ready for action. Tonight, it begins! Tonight! I leave, finally, Sunny Beach, in search of my manhood, the south, an order, my sanity, some other dream!*

*That is what shall happen!*

9

So in came James Olivier, famous chef, a cheeky grin, silly hat, helmet and oil.

Jesus! I thought. Here we go again! I'd rather deal with bad ass Ramses than this joker, I thought, as James began setting himself up in my kitchen here at Hey! Hey! Oi'lay! Where he has been contracted by our pretentious owners to- Show us how it's done, they wrote by V-Mail and text. I've never met the people that own this fucking place, despite being manager for ten years!

Oh well! I think. James is here now.

"Sorted!" he says, slinging a hefty dash of olive oil straight into a pan, sloshing it, adding fish-bits and...

Dribble! I muse, suddenly pleased at this circus.

"Have it!" dribbles podgy James, and I lean the weight of my corpse into my hips, an old habit of the overworked, as me and the team watch the mockney-cuddly-dough-faced hipster monkey cook his onions in lashings of grease at the expense of this cold dinner of a company. I prefer Ainsley, I consider, checking Chelsea's fine little ass. Big, black Ainsley, and his Cocaine habit, like mine- also at secret cost to this company, I muse, feeling better as James chirps, spits-

"Luverly!"

As he carries on, I watch the tele up on the far wall-corner instead- the life support machine. A most recent V-Mail from Head Office warned us the tele in the kitchen was on its way out, and that's probably thanks to meddling James, his TV Crew of utter bastards, it is reported.

I'm lucky the cameras aren't here tonight! The place could be better; Still, most of me crew are on hard drugs and that does tend towards damped efficiency- that and peanut wages. Still, the dough-monkey does it for the monkeys, and I watch an old episode of Jewels Holland's Music Show. Figgy Shitdust, in his prime, gives it- Catch A Falling Dickie-Bow, from his legendary, Everything album. Diddy Bop, his only hit-single comes soon after. His bright white puff, snarl of retribution and purple Les Paul, wriggle, slither and jig, awkwardly as he prattles through the songs, trying desperately to hide his Cocaine and Crunk habit, that would in time for his unreleased fourth album, turn to heroin again and kill him when he started dick-injecting. His sick relationship with Sid Nasty, shows, as he gives it the edgy punk-shocked finish it all needs, and Fig, finishes by lighting a snout with a shaking hand, as Jewels, that grin, allows with his giant hand, the crowd to uneasily applause, knowing that Everything was a fluke.

I return my attention to James, and realise it's a fluke the kitchen hasn't flooded in the buckets of oil he uses as more of his zealous-spittle hits steaming yellow grease and his head resembles more and more, pricked-uncooked-bread, as more secret Crunk, kicks in.

\*

"Thank you, Dave Webb, me' ol' mucker!" says James, two long, steamy, sizzle and drizzle over-easy hours later, slinging on his open-lid; as I shuffle him out the front doors shaking me keys, making it obvious.

"Thank you, Mr Olivier," I respond, doing the smile and waving to him as he leaves on his scooter. I check my phone- a message from that idiot, goth cousin of mine up north! Nutkins. What a wanker! I laugh, a quick line, and then I hear it! Bang! Crash! Wallop! Screams and commotion.

I take a peek.

It seems a truck has ended James' evening.

"Hmm," I ponder, remembering how soo many celebrity chefs

are mysterious dying recently! And why couldn't they have sent Rick Stein! At-least, Stein knows how to party, his disco in Cornwall and chip shop on the wall. He wouldn't have refused Absinthe, as goody-goody James, did; Well, now look at James! I sadden, but warm. "Tea-total, and so greasy he slipped under the wheels of a lorry!"

*

I take the tube back to Paradise Estate, where I live. There are a few tramps around, but not many, and as I pass the burning bins to the foyer, I am reminded that home is home after a long shift at Hey Hey.

What a fucking day! I stagger, up the steps because the lift is out of order, as it has been for many long weeks here now. The cause of this place is unknown, the estate, her people, our ways; and nothing seems to be able to stop it, though the addicts are rife, and howling as I find Level 42. And, like Mark King, I feel a lesson in love, as a Rustler's Pork And Grind, finds dinger, and then it all fades to black, after.

*

I awaken, phone buzzing.

"Cousin Nutkins! You what? Calm down!" I find my Eagles- this could be long, King-Size, even. "Dreams? Jim? What? Look, Big Jim's a wanker! Don't worry about it!" I try not to laugh as Nutkins tells me about how Jim put rats in his bedsheets last night and it gave him bad dreams. "For gawds sake, Nutkins! Get a grip!"

"Don't call me Nutkins!" he yells.

"Don't call me in the middle of the night, ye fag!" I goad him, snapping me phone shut.

Awoken, I stagger to the kitchen, still in me Oi'lay uniform, find a J-Dog-End, fire-it. She feels good, and hot, like the 3-Bar in the living room, the same room, Howling Harry, did himself with gas. The ghost of the old man still haunts, the council warned me, before putting me here after drug-addiction and bankruptcy. Thank Christ for Oi'lay! I sometimes wonder, though like Trainspotting said, tis grim, the workaday.

"Whack-A-Day!" I say aloud, remembering that it starts soon, at daybreak, and with no shift tomorrow, I am free to get high and watch Timmy, in me cacks, Mallet children.

\*

As Timmy hammers the little children, and the bleak, pale sun comes up, I consider Trevor! Trevor Skeletons, another relative I need to visit before Christmas! More time spent chasing family, and it amps-up from December the very first, or fourth, as it is, I am reminded as Mallet, ends and the Bumblebee Morning News, begins- that regional edge; images of men fighting, police brutality, crying babies and screaming, hair-pulling women, the tune baring close resemblance to the Police sirens, outside and Ambulance noises, the alarm-clocks of every quarter of an hour.

I scratch my balls. Pac-Man pants. I could get onto some Call Of Duty, but I really could use some kip. I get hold of me controller anyway, fire up the XX-BOXX. She humms, purrs, as the game gets right in there, my expensive We-Fe, really worth it!

As some ten year old starts mouthing-off already, I tell him to

Can-it!

"Fuck your mother, OilyGhost!"

OilyGhost, is my username, and abuser name, as I remind him- "Tickle your dead father's ball-sack!" Pleased with that one.

"Eat your mother's titties for trifles!" he retorts.

"Fuck off Geetle!" I tell him, firing off an instant head-shot, seconds in, from distance, laughing as XWarriorOwlBladeSoulX, loses some of his, and he curses at me in high-pitched school-boy vocals. "Go take a brown owl!" I taunt him. "Lose some of that arse-hole weight around ye!"

"Fuck you paedo!" he screams back. "Get a job, loser!" and I have to agree, that one stung.

"I got a job, chucky cheese!" I shout, suddenly losing my rag. "I'm a fucking restaurant manager! How do like that?" And he laughs at me, making it worse, as other children laugh too and I rage quit.

## 10

"Get to painting penis!" Roy, screams at me down the phone, Jackal, glaring at me, piles of cash for bedding on his/my couch.

"But..."

"Don't argue Kevin. Just begin painting cock," Roy continues seriously.

"But..."

"And I shall send a car for you both in the morning- There is a development in the teddy saga."

"What..."

"Sadistic cunts!" Roy barks. "They're getting worse! Berty lost an arm on Chinese New Year! Ye! They said they wanted to play a game with him too, after beating me; so while I was out

Celebrating with my kind, the teddys removed his arm with a cleaver, sealing the wound with a flaming steak, as they threatened they would do as was done to the Spik, in, Day Of The Dead, should he lose, they wrote. And, boy! Did he lose!"

"My God!" I splutter, genuinely appalled but, Chiao, had already hung-up. "You won't believe what the teddys have done to poor Berty!" I whine to Jack, attempting to clean the dirty U2 with a dish-cloth, Eagle, on.

"Gang-raped him? He'd like that!"

"No! *Berty!* Not Roy!"

"What!"

"An arm and a cock!"

\*

Me and Jack, sit in Roy's office- he's beaming, and on the desk in front of him is a hamper. "Guess what's in these?" he says, sounding almost, and resembling a yellow-Asian, Vincent Price, but staying more Ming.

"What?" asks Jack.

"Sandwiches?" I faux-ask, knowing what is really in there, not liking it.

"These, Gentlemen, are Penis-Flesh Pies!" He lifts the lid, revealing many tasty looking pies; thick, yellow crust, meaty waft. "And these are but a sample, from my special bakery! I have many more for our guests on opening night, many- some even for Gator Tool, his new girlfriend, *my Veronica!* Yes! I have some for them too! Now, to tasting!" he beams, plucking one, bringing it slow to his goatee-gash, allowing his long, vampire teeth deep into the soft pie, eyeballing us both at the same time as he tongues the human flesh of a man's cooked penis that is inside.

I shudder.

Jack, chuckles.

"Hmmm," noises Chiao, clearly in some form of twisted-ecstacy- "*He* tastes *soo* good!" he says with his mouth full, grinning from pointy-ear to ear. "Come here, Berty! Give me a hand!" he bark-beckons-mocks, his old, one-armed assistant, blood-stained dish-rag-stump and look of absolute misery. "*These* will put some lead back in that old pencil! An arm for a dick?" he cackles, some flesh falling from his mouth. "Stop being gloomy!"


11


In I go, Roy Chiao's Weird Arts of Las Alberto! After a Christmas gift for Cousin Nutkins, who shall be visiting after suffering another mental breakdown, so his ridiculous mother told me over the phone. And, while I enjoy mocking, Clarence Nutkins Skeletons, from Sunny Beach, up North, I also care for him in a strange way, having grown up with the wanker! And, while Nukins, never grew up, or left home, I did both, and enjoy mocking him and feeling less of the old loser I really am- especially around Christmas Time, miserable Christmas, when no-one, not even my own elderly mother wishes to visit me, I never weep, as alcohol and video games, fast-food and other pleasures eliminate all of those emotional things, I chose not not acknowledge.

Down I go.

The steps are narrow, steep, completely inaccessible to the disabled, elderly or retarded, I marvel, already liking this place I read about in Time Off! They have an exhibition starting here next February entitled Penis, and I was curious about the sinister little

Chinese Fella who runs the gaff.

I don't mind Art *Galleys*. One of the perks of the City- that and bars, and clubs, and many taxis. Though Las Alberto, is a shit-hole, there are pockets of pretty, fun-coloured art, and I chose to paint my day off in her oily paint-pot, I did on Roy, much Crunk taken today.

\*

He springs from the black shadows. "This is Elisabeth Ashley's, Mutley Chunter- her latest. Tis about a man who enjoys scat, and tea in the afternoon in Summer."

"That's nice. No. I'm looking for something more disturbing," I remark, eyeballing little Roy, his purple Ghi, etc. He points his cane towards somewhere, says-

"This way, sir!"

\*

"The Man Who Sucks His Own Cock," slings Roy, revealing her majesty with a claw.

"I will take it!" I say, knowing how much Nutkins will love this.

\*

"I had a lot of fun bringing this son-of-a-bitch home today!" I tell black fatty Diddy Pop, on the Bluetooth, skinning-up on the little coffee-table, having bagged some weed too on the way back. I fire her up, inhale, grin, exhale. "I got a free pork pie with it! What about you?"

"Scammin'!"

"Oh." I think I can hear Diddy, spinning tunes in his bedroom, but I can't be sure. "When's yer next Disco?"

"Saturday. Two-weeks."

I admire my new painting, rather expensive, but worth it, on the wall. The skinny black man, sucking himself off, in Oil.

"Yer a fucking Gaylord!" Diddy tells me, having told him in detail of my new picture, meant for Nutkins, maybe for me, for Christmas. "Aye! You've got a point! It could give out gay vibes, this one!" I wonder, suddenly alarmed, never wishing to oppose possible one-nighters in my condo of squalour with a *gig*-glaring homo-suspicion point.

Paradise Estate.

"Well, I think you've spoiled it!" I tell Diddy.


## 12


It was in The Beagle, right before Noel, that things got interesting, as I, David Webb, hooked up with old pal, and bassist, Joe Giblet, and with Diddy, we set up another record shop, as Giblet's music career failed, when Max Silvers, lead-vocalist and guitarist of one-album-wonder, Rad Stallion, passed-on, from drugs and alcohol, his big, ex-forces heart, giving-out, and effectively separating the band, as their Manager and producer, respectively, died too, from hard drugs and old age.

In respect of Joe's old record store, we re-named the new one, Better Days, in the same old location -Number 5- redecorated, buying and selling vinyl, like the old days, and kicking-it, as old men, on the grim, colourful streets of Las Alberto! Old-London!

*

What a fucking touch! I wrote to managers of Hey Hey, via text and V-Mail. Living like a fucking king, I am! Doing nothing, listening to records, getting paid, hanging-out with friends, getting drunk every day. Best of luck without me- I'm sure one of the Snowflake-Millienials will do a spiffing job! Bye!

Nutkins wanted in on the fun, but I sent him gently packing back up north, where he would go on to lose his shit and summon demons that would kill the town! "What a goth-tosser!" I say to myself, as I click on more COD, and Diddy strolls in with bundles of Fillet o' Fish, on special at McDonald's, real Cod, in a soft bun and creamy white Tartare Sauce.

13

On the player, The Cramps, give it. The afternoon is late and the air is sleazy. It's kick-out, at the school, and Dave watches the schoolgirls. Black, Diddy P, has his feet up, and no-one is in the shop, indeed the rain has brought an added sorrow to 5 Lord Albert Street, where Bumblebees have buzzed the last few days as the weather gave sweet relief after further usual rain.

And then there was the snow!

And then old Roy!

Prison!

After what he called, an innocent act of art, in court, to no avail as the judge and jury proceeded to nail his skinny, whipped little Chinese ass! The ugly streets flow with the rain-blood of recent drama, and penis-flesh, on the minds and lips of locals, who stare, glare, look at each other down The Parade, and at the station, The Gates, where old men scatter, and old women natter.

And I miss Max, the band! The drunk nutter!

Rat, passes sometimes, has starting collecting again, rare old soul, metal and a dash of fusion, as are his solitary needs. I tell him to get involved with another band, a new project, but he says he's over the hill, and it is true- we are older, each!

But the shop, Better Days, has a newness about it, a smell, a freshness in the air, that unique, unmistakable fragrance of masses upon masses of vinyl. Walls stacked, the beginnings of order, the realisation of chaos, and we have left some piles to simply collapse, and clients swim in it.

"Tell us about Sally Doll," Dippy goads me.

"Fuck off!" I tell him, as usual. "I'm a closed book on that subject! I never want to talk about Sally Doll!" I finish, serious.

*

"You never let em' in the house," referring to Tramps, and the one who used to live out the back, in the creepy garden, in a shed, back in the day. It's still out there, I can see it, via a cracked back window in the un-renovated back-end of the building. Tall, creeping weeds, thick, black and green pervade, a few dead skeletons of older trees, old as the marshes these lands once were; the broken rooftop of the lonely shed, or witches cottage, as I used to call her; and she is still out there, on the mini-marsh of the garden here at 5 Lord Albert Street, a place of history, black and seed. "You can feed them, chat with them, but you never let them in the house!"

\*

"Turn it up!" I shout, as Chav And Dave's Dirty Last Christmas, finds needle, yet again. Old Mrs Browns Dirty Knickers, is followed by, Cheer Up! Eileen! Sit On Me Face! And though it is not Christmas, any-more, as Spring blooms, it is a good record to perk up to on a quiet rainy afternoon. The finale, I Got Pink Crackers Full Of Egg-Nog For Ye! Made the drinks come out again, to one or two passing customer's merriment, mild-shame, though neither bought anything, just drank our Sherry.

The car smoking outside as records change belongs to Diddy, a piece of shit his father gave him, as Huffstuffingpuff, gives me endless money as I need it these days unquestioningly. Dave Webb, ex-restaurateur, and lazy tosser, is a quiet, unassuming person, as he does DJ duties, J on, and has indeed spider's webs tattooed on each of his elbows. His lank, greasy hair, is long, like mine, and his beard, ratty, grey, like mine too. Black Diddy, has an afro, and is fat and bejewelled, and single-childed, like most of his kind around here are. He is constantly driving to the take-away, particularly Pizza-Box, McDonald's, Burger-Time or Bra-Kebab-Ra, round' the block, 27/7, and is always on the phone to his dealer or ex, for a scream-up.

*

Later on, I cruise on me Low-Rider. We growl through the streets, sometimes setting-off the car alarms of weak parked cars as I click and shift down through her gears.

Stopped at the red.

Chunky wheels stabilise her in the night-drizzle that snakes down my visor. Crap visibility, just how we like it, I muse, rocking her into first, sliding off into the night leaving cars behind, the veins slippery, wet.

Oh, Sally Doll, you cunt, I anger, weaving her between traffic on the main, dangerous but in control. The sky leaks more night, and I like it like that, older now, wiser perhaps, riding again, a quality machine, like I deserve.

*

At a late night Greasy Dave's, I stop for a fried-egg roll, the Snooker on the tele. Some are drunk, some are homeless, one is probably gay, I consider, stood, waiting as Gladys, who worked once at Nasty Fucking Records, gets the coffee while Dave does me egg and Scot's man Hendry paints Davis, Steven. "I'm not surprised you lot never made it! And I'm not surprised Sid did himself in, either! A right sicko!"

"You leave him alone, Gladys! Let him rest in peace with the others!"

"And as for you! What you did to Sal!"

"That isn't true, Gladys!"

"I eard' they found her in your attic, her arms and legs cut off, kept in a box!"

"If that were true I'd be in prison!"

"Well, we all know you killed her!" she gloats, firing one up, forgetting my coffee. "It's only a matter of time before the truth surfaces, and you go down! It's OK, long-hair; there's plenty of Gays in prison, just dying to get into you! Rock-Star! A Raw, Red rusty Sherri-ff, more like! And puddles of bloody semen!"

\*

The ride back to Paradise Estate is short as I speed through the quieter streets of blacker hours. Gladys is a foul creature! I wonder, as I park up. The burning bins burn bright tonight, and in those flames, her face, Sally, undeniable, there.

I shudder.

Move hastily up the tower block, into me cave.

What the hell did happen to you, Sally Doll? I wonder, feeling the pain again, the not-knowing- my child!

Did she have she/he?

I have only questions, and questionable heart-ache. Sometimes I wonder that her disappearance is a blessing; she was an awful person in a way, yet I loved her, I thought, and maybe I still do? I consider, finding whiskey, clicking the tele.

## 14

"David Webb?"
"Yeah."

Who's this geezer, I wonder, eyeballing the old man in the suit; probably as old as me, but seems a lot older, and certainly more serious.

"I'm Ned Skeletons, a friend of Clarence!"

"Oh, aye! I thought I recognised you. You've had a hair cut and a beard trim! Do you still live in a mobile library?"

"No! The house was destroyed the night Morg..."

"The monster that killed the town!"

"Yes!"

\*

In Buckstar coffee-place, Old Ned, hands me a file full of papers. "These were Clarence's. He wanted you to have them, he said before they put him in the mental asylum."

"Oh."

"Yes. Poems, songs, drawings and things."

"Any money?"

"No. Clarence was broke right till' the end!"

"Oh."

\*

Weedeater, give it; Diddy, cleans his grinder, readies a THC crystal carrot! "There be snow on dem mountains!" he chuckles, sprinkling mother-nature's dandruff all over tobacco, as I peruse Nutkin's writings.

"What a lot of nonsense!" I say, putting them down, except for a picture he did, in pencil-crayon, a gay dragon. "Poor old Nutkins, really was a nut-job!"

"Yeah! Who was that creepy man in an ill suit?" asks Joe, sat with his bass, sat on his amp in the corner. A snout dangles from his beard, as it often does despite us and customers reminding him of the smoking ban in places such as these- shops.

"That was a loose family member from up north," I tell him, firing one myself, reading the Bumblebee, pictures of starving tramps. "He's relocating to Old-London, after Cousin Nut-Job summoned a sea-monster that killed the town! These are his writings and drawings! Very strange! Strange! Like the taste of this Pork Pie I got at the art Galley?"

"The meat looks grey," says Joe.

"So it does," I say, killing the harsh, salty, very-meat flavour with more of Joe's viscous red wine. "Fire-up the lava-lamp, would you, Joe? And get the coffee-pot back on, would ye? Diddy, turn this off! Put on some Jazz!"

\*

When the bus crashed outside, people ran screaming, my head spinning after another afternoon of heady wine and hard drugs, I look up, remember exactly which one of us three old men I am.

Joe Giblet.

Damn!

And amidst the screams I am reminded that I am invited to dinner with Lord Huffstuffingpuff, my elderly, insane father, this evening at Le Bistro, up-town.

Damn!

Worse than time with Uncle Gregoire, I ponder, getting up to view the wreckage outside.

"I keep witnessing crashes!" moans Dave.

"This doesn't look good," I compliment, viewing, through the smoke, the grim reveal of a head-on, car meets bus, at mid-speed, but fast enough to crumple car, where passenger is squashed, fat and screaming, face covered in blood, she is, people already filming with their phones, the sounds of an argument.

"Women drivers!" goads Diddy, his feet up at the desk, firing his mini-bong chaser.

*

"They dragged her out in the end- well, more cut her out with massive buzz-saws as she screamed in shock and terror!" I tell Puffy. He sits there, at our usual table here at Le Bistro, where we come once a month, if he is lucky- and tonight, with the need for frippery, steak and fine red wine, served by another human, he is lucky!

"How was the bus?" he asks, his nose bright purple, wig, pin-stripes, red-rose and eyes like craters.

"A bit crumpled at the front- Driver had a big beer belly that must have cushioned him. One old lady fell and knocked all her front teeth out, someone told me later in the pub. She's suing, apparently! Speaking of which, or the witch! How's mother?"

"Dying, hopefully. That old bitch just keeps on living, making my life hell from afar! She's been spotted recently at the sailing club; my favourite spot these days! Old cunt turned up the other night, giving it Champs and Hell!"

"At-least she's still mobile!"

"No! She was in her wheelchair, her crew of assistants! Despicable woman!"

"That's my mummy!"

"She's a cunt! And you're better off keeping away from her!"

"That's what she said about you!"

"She would. More wine?"
"Yes."

## 15

There was a foul stank that eminated from the basement, one day- a place none of us have really bothered about since our arrival here at 5 Lord Albert, Better Days, that so far, have been a bit better than the last few years when each of us lost it all; and, I suppose that that is the bond that keeps us three together, here at the record shop, down-town, London, stinking of dead fish. "One of us needs to get down there, have a look!"

Dave, comes over, takes a sniff. "Jesus Haddock! Call in the proffesionals! That's fucking rank!"

\*

"Yeah! You got a rat problem!" the rat-faced handy-man says. "Big fucking rats down there, and a dead body!"

"Do what?" I say.

"Yeah! The corpse of a woman! Decomposing into slime!"

"Joe!" Dave, says. "That ain't Sally, is it?" and Diddy laughs.

"Fuck you! And no!"

\*

I sit at the bus stop watching a puddle of fresh puke. The bus is late, the traffic thick, for it is Christmas.

I hate this fucking place, I think, looking forward only to a polite chat with my Job Councillor, and jolly glow she lays on for the losers, us.

I detest this life they made, their mental system.

We, the losers, they call us- certainly the jobless, wifeless over 40 ones, like me.

Mad, they sometimes label us.

Broke.

And then it hits me, like a ton a shit.

Absolutely no hope.

Nothing.

## 16

Sunny Beach
Watershed Bay

April 1st 2017
06.30AM

The grey of the morning seeped out of the night-black, revealing the stretch of North Sea, a misty horizon. That mist had been there for days now; and in that deeper grey, the outline of a fishing trawler as it chugged slowly back to port after another long night. On that Trawler, Betty II, Captain Maddock, one of the crustiest old fisherman left in the area, maintained her steady course home, one hand on the wheel, a cigarette, and a keen eye as they went through the mist, where the only evidence of day, was a brighter fog.

On the beach, Albert, the old man, watched that boat emerge from the distance, wondering about the mist, for it was a dank mist, that had brought with it something ominous; a feeling. A feeling, Albert, had felt once or twice in his long life, and a feeling he could not ignore. It had brought him to the beach this morning- up before sunrise, hectic dreams and a jolt awake, impossible to ignore, the feeling *there*.

No. He hadn't even had breakfast yet, not even a cup of tea. The beach, this bay had been his only intention, get home, lay a brown egg, bacon-butty, sleep; and as he stood there alone, he wondered exactly what that *other* intention might be? The weird one, *noir*, lost in the mist and strange in his old mind. Yet, he was old enough, wise enough to know how my*s*eriously the Good Lord worked, and was already resolved to the idea of returning home that morning, none the wiser, wiser.

And that was when he saw it; a ripple, movement in the quiet ocean before him, some distance out but noticable.

He rubbed his eyes as the surface of the water was disturbed once again, an electric ripple in the grey; and something emerged- a fin? A tail? Shiny, seal-skin!

And it was over.

*

Joyce Maple, was buttering toast when she saw the old man, Albert, shuffle past her kitchen window, Duffel-Coat. "Where's he going this time of day? What's he up to?" she asked her dog, Pepper, being nosy, as usual- a *curtain-twitcher*, some had labelled her, and Joyce, had reasoned that it wasn't her fault; a widow of three years now, sometimes bored, lonely if she was forced to admit it, as she had to Doctor Staples, once or twice. "It is only normal that a person who lives on their own, looks out of the window a lot!" she had reasoned with the Doctor, knowing somewhere that she was probably kidding herself.

"Join a local club," Staples, had advised her.

"I am disliked around here," she had told him.

"Hmm," the Doctor, had noised, knowing of her complaining neighbours, all of which had labelled her a trouble-maker, a nuisance. Sunny Beach, was a large-enough town to remain relatively anonymous, if you kept yourself to yourself, but small enough for news, gossip and rumours to travel faster than speeding-bullets, of which real ones, fortunately were rare, if not non-existent in the area.

A Raven, perched suddenly on her windowledge- a black-beast of a bird, beak as sharp as her dead husband's razor; "An omen?" she panicked, as Pepper began barking, jumping, going nuts. The Raven gave her one beady eye before taking flight, wings flopping, ocean direction.

*

Albert, passed through town like a ghost. Misty, sombre, Sunny Beach, was quiet, even as folk began waking. He passed Sunny Cafe, *Old Mather*, the pub, cut up through Bishop's Lane, then right across the high street where commercial businesses such as

Wallworths, would be opening soon. And at the top of the hill, on run-down King's Road, he disappeared into his red-brick little semi-detached, front and side windows hidden by overgrown shrubbery. He preffered it that way, and valued his privacy, certainly in his older years, the things he had witnessed in his former, working life, the dreaded mines; King's Road, had been his home for several years now, and tucked-up at the back of Sunny Beach town, it was ideal for his solitary needs.

The Postman, had already been, and Albert, shuddered when he saw that shaky ink of handwriting that formed his address. Groaning, feeling his back, *feeling* the feeling, he bent down to pick it up, knowing who it was from.

Dr Dragon Noir.

Tyr.

\*

Chief Baker, finished getting into his uniform. His wife, Freda, was downstairs fixing breakfast, the sounds of pans rattling, the radio. In the mirror, his fifty-two years didn't upset him as much as it had recently; the death of Alice, or Saggy Alice, had weighed heavy on him somehow, a town that wanted answers, always wanted something- and he loved it here somehow. Some detectives from a bigger town, a city nearby were still on the case, weeks on from the shocking discovery of her corpse, swinging from a high-beam in her stately home, now crumbling *into Mather*, Blithe House.

He slicked his moustache, adjusted his collar. There was going to be more of that story today, he supposed, finding a grimace, a familiar reflection, a pen, his pocket.

*Dragon Noir.*

It hit him like a sledgehammer, he felt for his chair, sat down, loosened his collar, took deep breaths.

"You OK? Chief?"

"No."

## 17

Tyr Castle
AD 5

The victim swirled his halls, the fly in his web, and he watched her from the black shadows of his halls and dungeons, turrets, towers, toilets and long, psychedelic corridors where she fled in a daze, virtually helpless, bare-foot in her silk, white-nightie, that flowed like milk around the curves of her body as she ran for her life, occasionally sweeping her perfect hair to one side.

Count Dragoir, watched her.

Two, bat-red-eyes.

He crept behind her, smelt her, occasionally tickled her with a long finger, teased her with his unique cosmic horror and death. "Where have you come from?" he calls to her, in his charming voice from everywhere.

"What am I doing here? What do you want from me?" she screams, breaking down, and he heeds her flood of tears, appearing behind her in the candlelit shadows of this impossibly long corridor, a thousand doors, and no way out.

As his fangs pushed through his gums, the blood-honey need within him insatiable, his eyes wide, blood-shot, hungry and ready, and oh, how she screamed as he went deep into her neck, his long claws restraining her, penis hard, vagina wet, for indeed, Dragoir was not only the Count Of Counts, before The Keeper, finally rescued the castle, but he was also the universe's first hermaphrodite! Yes, he was!

*

"But there are worse stories than that!" Old Granny tells me, and I want to pull her beard, but last time I did, she stretched me and it hurt terribly. She has very strong claws too, and... well, I don't mess with Granny.

*

And someone said she went to sleep- A wizard, told us. Q. I am.
Strange.
Aznd then there was the AZ, Orb deal.
Reyna.
Where the hell am I now?

*

And somewhere, Mark 2 Doom-Bots malfunctioned.
2069!

18

*Scroll 158675000*
*Writer- Darius Cal*
*Concerning Cluster*
*Borealis-Cosmia*
*Cosmia-Gallactic*
*For Elders, Shines and Yaa.*

*In response to your call, and havin g heard from her majesty*
  *golden-seal*

2069.

*What to say about 2069? What happened was true- all of it, all of the bizarre stuff before it, a watershed of madness. Movies foresaw it, music heard it coming, just as terrifying as being there.*
*D-Day.*
*They couldn't turn thazt one back on earth, I remember, going through my many ancient tomes here at the castle. Somewhere in the eaves, down the passages, brick and echoing, candlelit with ink nighmares, The Count, Dragoir, tries on more of his dresses, his skins.*
*He is a very sick room-mate.*
*"I want to fuck you," he told me the other night over dinner, his voice hideously near despite the long, long table in the dining-chamber, our opposite ends.*
*His ways sicken me, yet...*
*He has been lurking here for such a long time, making my writing odder, my spelling bad, the deepest dungoens I sent him in his coffin. Somehow, a length of passage of time, agao, he founde his waye up, he did, and has bought an unholy something or other new, from that basement, deeeep*

*deep*
*here at the tower.*

## 19

The Space.
Vega.
New Paradise 324.
2069 – Earth Date
06.30AM Local Time.
The sun, King-Sun, came up on a very strange planet, right on time. Burning in the shadows, the almighty giantess of the sun, this behemoth cosmic, very ancient sun had been waiting a very long time recently during Dark Nebula, to spill her orange glory, her juice all over a fresh morning, an Un-Cursed One, as they had been named as they sprung; *Spring*, some would have said, the Humans certainly.

Vega.
New Paradise.
A New Age, in Space.

"A new paradise!" declared Lord Epithelium, a short while ago in recent history as the planet officially entered the Black Dragon Space Belt of Cosmia-Gallactic and Cluster Boundaries. BDSPCG and CB, it was called, in short, on Earth, Headquarters of SC and Shine-Forces.

There was now a mysterious new Cosmic problem, one, even Earth-human, Conrad Von-Rancour, would write about in his eponymous book, 4, many moons and sh-rooms ago.

That very strange problem had been titled, 4.

"Four More!" declared Elders, in hasty response to worried scrolls from Darius Cal, The Keeper, his castle, his Island in the middle of space, Verboten, The Orb. "There are four more scrolls to be writ before She, will ever wake up again!" they wailed. "Her sleeping is not a gift, oe a good omen!" They declared. "It is a curse!"

20

"Raise your lips!" I tell Beepo. "Go on! Raise em so I can smack em!" I tell him.

"Fuck off Mario!" he tells me, and I almost reach for my Lazer-Gun, finish him off, instead, I finger her cold steel, instead, and excite my very, old man's penis, that still works thanks to future medicine, technology, Bio-Mechanics, will-power, money and arrogance; fortunately, even as an old man, Mario Star, Me, still has all that, unlike old-pal, Beepo, who I'm surprised stuck-around, to be honest. He's had some work done, but nothing like me, who has had the works, and still looks good, I reason; sometimes I think I look a bit like Harrison, in his last Wars movie, and have certainly stolen his wardrobe. Beepo, an alien, is sort-of like hair-less Chewbacca, companion nonetheless; Or do I tolerate him? I wonder, twirling noodles.

Tonight it is Beepo's 85th birthday, the old squid, his flappy-wide lips, that never fail to amuse me; he finds it hard to suck, so I have deliberately taken him to a noodle-bar this evening, after the first hot-spring day in ages. Beings seem happier for a change, here on Vega, Lazy-Vega, the real El-Dorado! Where all the really-rich live, often literally laughing and joking at the poor as we hang-out at fancy bars and restaurants all the time.

It is exceptional, this planet! A real catch! Unlike some of the things I have caught in the past, as a reporter, my miserable fucking former life I wouldn't shit on, even if I had to. "Hey

Beepo! Let's hit up the casino tonight!" I offer him, twirling a cocktail-mixer, surprised they even do fresh cocktails here at the noodle bar, where generic Asian Earth-Human-Robots perform all sorts of Tea-Pan-Yakky, or something, spinning and twirling, like yellow circus monkeys, all happy and sociable, and better, because they are artificial so you don't have to tip them like the real ones, who always look out for that. "Dance monkeys!" I shout at one, clapping at his wok and shovel, and he doesn't even frown. "That's it, dance! God, I love this place," I tell Beepo. "You know, *why* they never made a movie out of The Underfoot Ripper, I'll never know! They missed a tick there!"

"Trick!"

"Wha?"

"TRICK!" he yells.

"Alright, flabby lips!" I retort, waving a chop-stick at him. "Dogs do tricks, and maybe... No," I conclude, deciding not to ask one of the Asian robot-chefs to do a trick. They already have their hands full with Tea-Pan-Yakky, I conclude, warm in my inner-generosity and fairness of reason. Discipline, I would label it if I could note it in my little note-pad, pen? The good-old days of reporting, The Daily Space; Sandy, Editor, Little Richard Pickle, and Beepo, I think, eye-balling him. "Beepo! What specie are you exactly again?" I ask him.

"Squid," he tells me.

"No, I said what are you, not what you're eating!" pleased at how good at jokes I am. "Ha!" I noise at him, poking his funny lips with my chinky-stick, the end of my penis out on purpose. I love how the old fella worries the little real human Chinkys, who scatter and scream when, after a few hits of Spicy-Rice, he perks up secretly under the table. Then, I take him for the long walk to the restrooms, allowing him to tip and curtsy my fellow diners. Because I am old now, I get away with it every time, every place I go, and it warms my cold, black dead heart. Sometimes he even cries at the nasty ones who don't like him. Real, thick yellow tears he shakes at them!

To be continued...

    I thought, and then the waiter arrived with more. "F*y*ck!" I wobble, very drunk. "It's good here, eh Beepo?"
    "What?"
    "It's good here!"
    "Yes. Wery!" And I laugh at the way he pronounced very, noodles falling from his wide lips like pasta-water, from a waterfall.
    "Say something else with your mouth full," I ask him, quite glad of Beepo, this evening. Better than Biggles! Ginger Biggles! A more dangerous companion than Silver Buckstar, many moons ago. Despite his age, Ginger Biggles, is probably worse than me. Even I find myself embarrassed at the antics of Biggles, that sleazy leather flying cap, monocle. "Ginger! He is the gayest of them all!" I tell Beepo, as the waiter goes away. "His plum jokes and senility!"
    "What?"
    "Yes, Biggles. An Ex-Star Raider, always banging on about war, and coming close to sexual-harassment thingys. I brought him here once but he started to play invaders with his genitalia. They called the police! I'm surprised they haven't recognised me, to be honest. Ha! We left in a hurry, Ginger Biggles, pills gone, arms out, flying his imaginary Raider out the hatch, clothes-lining one of the little chinky women on the way out, he did, screaming, like the noise his ship used to make!"

21

Mars City Central.
2069
Mayor Tool, was drunk again at Mars Elections, where everyone wondered if this creature could really win again? Mayor! Again? Most thought, but going along with it. He was a curious creature with strange energy. That night he was giving it his full South-African at the bar, again, bright red cheeks, bulging eyes, pint of piss and prawns. "Ye! I ad' me dinkle out n' wus sprayin' the tables, wen' I, Amanda! Mad Pissed we was, id' was laquer! Then this woman came in, covered in blood n' spoiled id! Said her husband had just had is' brains blown out in the carpark! Id spoilt me joke, it did n' I told em' id' appens' all da time, it does, me big dick still in me hands, getting down off table-top!"

Amanda sighs. She's heard this one before.

"Yee! So I told her she woz lucky she weren't in the Soetto! He woulda got a rubber tire n a match! I laughed at her! Ye! They chuck the tyres over yuh n' set fire to ye! Brutal id is! Head shot's like a cheese sandwich, round ere it is, I said n' everyone laughed!"

22

Black Chilly and his Pet Wolf, is not a man you want to cross. He runs the casino I frequent, Dem Niggas, it is called, and though it is violent, it is also local, The Underfoot Arena, department of Mars City Central, I have always lived.

Black Chilly, seems pleased to see me. "My nigga!" he says, flashing me a gold tooth, his gold cane, gold top hat, Star sunglasses, many rings, things, accessories, and kinky boots. His long, startling red sequin Top-Coat, sparkles like the moon planets of far, hot clusters, and how he shines!

"My nigga, to you!" I say, shaking his hand before he pulls a gun on me and BLAM!

I wake up.

Sigh.

It was just one of those dreams again. One of those Chilly Nigger dreams I have been having. Dreams that have plagued me all my life. Somehow, with the on-set, creeping death inevitable, certainly considering my on-going life-style choices, I am grateful of those dreams now I live in Paradise.

Yes, I had the last laugh, as-

Dreams and bad memories of the past only serve me to be grateful of what I have now, I remind myself, sick of positivity.

It is true.

I do somehow miss the grime, grunge, sludge and pain of Mars City Central, the really bad part. Editor, a stones throw over the massive sprawling chaos, in the offices always, even now, years later, The Daily Space. And I'm certain she misses me; at-least, on mornings as these, a hangover as wicked as thus, then certainly it comforts me to wonder that it caused her pain not to marry me. Her imaginary pain, in my warped mind, makes me feel honey-warm, as the dizzying effects of dehydration, and many cocktails, spins me into a snuggle of the soft pillow, cosy mattress and clean, white sheets I have here at my Pod.

What the hell happened last night?

It is a familiar consience question, at the usual moment in proceedings, and I give my mind a quick search just in case.

Ouch!

It seems I drank more of the glowing blue stuff I am addicted to than I expected. There is nothing inside my own skull except pain, black-treacle, mist and dust. And I'm starving, the number 4

suddenly there again, getting in the way of gut.
4
There was something inside that skull just a moment again. Number Four, I ponder, but it hurts too much again, so I stop that, and move my attention right back down the tube, into my gut.

Hang on!

There was something in there, the forest that is in there.

The Mountain Man!

It is he who has been haunting me most recently, more than crazy Biggles, that fucking hat. "I wonder if under his leather flying cap, Ginger Biggles, is actually ginger?" I ask the ceiling, perfect, not a single crack, just smooth, soft rich plaster. "Mountain Man, mystery man of the mountains and deep forests, would have him with his long, savage spear!" I giggle, pausing, as pain finds the cranium sharp.

And then, out through my throat comes the tip of that very spear, like Friday The 13$^{th}$, and I gargle, stunned as Tom Savini's hairy hand grabs my throat from under the bed, blood spurting everywhere!

I wake up!

Just another little dream. I had a snooze, as it is Sunday, or *Sundae*, as I prefer to call it, as I will most certainly be eating fresh, Italian Ice-Cream, later on this afternoon, near The Lagoon, after lunch. "Hmm," I muse, feeling my penis stiffen. "Shall I have English Roast, this lunch, or Mandarin?" I query, tickling my shaft with the ends of my slender fingers, writer's fingers- the fingers, soft-fingers of a man who has never done any manual labour.

\*

On Earth, they have Big Rising Stars, with Simon Scowl. Here, on Mars, we have Jizz In Their Eyes, hosted by Simon's son,

Treacle, and featuring the likes of Bad-Boy Beadle, Mayor Tool, on the panel. The Pole Dancers are always lucky to have gotten this far, and on tonight's show, I watch this morning, taped from last night, my secret love, Sheba, débuts. Boy, does she put on a show! I recognise many of her moves, and she throws in a few new ones for good measure.

Sweet bendy Sheba!

A Desert Cat Of Mars, and Beadle grins, wicked that eye and pincers. Rag-Doll Osborne, gives her another harsh lip-stick grin and two thumbs up, and as the audience cheer, Treacle makes the night complete by pressing his big red buzzer, a wry scowl.

I crawl out of bed and head for the shower. "I knew she'd make it!" I say, stepping into the shower-pod. The water is warm, perfect, instantly, unlike the plumbing troubles I had in my last Condo, The Underfoot A..

I pause.

I need to stop thinking about that place. I need to move on now, completely- allow myself fully to Vega, her rich fruits exotic. When, recently, they reduced the number of women and children allowed here, the place became almost perfect, Utopia, in my opinion- and barely a Boglin, in-fact, the few Boglins I have seen have been the intellectual, snob ones who keep themselves to themselves, are nothing like the regular shitty-prolaterian Boglin, we all dislike.

There is a little local problem with Yaa, her tribe of Dog Men and War-Lizards. But we tend not to worry about that as Paradise 324, is well guarded, with walls. That lot tend to be quiet these days anyway, up in hills far away, part of the universal Dragon thing, I have little knowledge or interest in. No. I'm only interested in living out my final, remaining life in comfort, and excess.

4

It is the best-selling brand of space-shroom, manufactured by the same team who scienced The Silver Sasquatch brand, that revolutionised a great many things. Then came 4. Found deep in Space, after disecting the strange code from the book of the same title written by mentalist, *scientist* Conrad Von-Rancour. When they *cracked* his book they found the best shroom they never imagined, and like Sasquatch, it once again changed everything.

For a while, my shroom-brand of choice was Killer Crocodile, but even I had to change over when I tasted the pleasures, and the sweet-pain, of 4. And when there was indeed an surprise invasion of killer giant crocodiles, whom came up from the sewers hungry and sick of space-rats, the brand-name was deemed distasteful after the hundreds of deaths that day until the army could flame them.

To be continued
next year

I thought, and then I remembered that strange little book I wrote a few years back that made me another fortune-

The Dank, The Dirty.

Four words in the title? I wonder, feeling a hung-over, opium-induced Da-Vinci code moment, seeing Hanks, not liking it much to be honest. A very clever man. "And there were four big rats on the front cover of that bastard!" I tell no-one. "Four big, hairy rats!"

"SLACK MOTHERFUCKER!" Superchunk shouts at me from the record player.

"Fuck off!" I tell them, loving them, loving the yellow cover I look at, the yellow-crunk gold morning that is falling like breakfast flakes, healthy ones with bright white fresh milk, from a happy cow.

Night Creatures.

They remind me what I am, really, as I rub my eyes, missing rain, storms, days on end of rain. And night. Rich black night, where it's soo nice.

I almost reach for my electric guitar, fire her up, not really knowing what to do next as more crispy flakes fall. "How clean they have made the air here!" I wonder, instead, falling back into my grey, designer, Phil Starkey. "Maybe I should write another book?" I consider, supping cafe, plump dressing gown, fresh flowers, maid brought. "Nah!" I decide, getting up to go to the toilet.

Pissing from my arse again, random squirts that interestingly hold no pain, I wonder what to do about Biggles today. He is interested in a round of Crazy-Gold, as it is known- much like Crazy-Golf, yet in this, the rich play only on a solid gold course, offering a very roly-challenge. The drinks are made of gold too, and some wager it is worth it only for the drinks, as, as a sport, most agree that it is rather shit. Some have taken to the human game, Snooker, where Human-Man, Ol' Rockin' Rocket-Ronnie, as he is known still knocks em' around like it's a game of dumb-pool, and still has outbursts, angry wavers in his focus, certainly now, in Space, and at his enhanced old-age. Fortunately, copious women and drugs help keep Ron, calm, on track, on pocket, and sometimes out of it! He has been threatened on many occasions to stop losing his riches to insane marriages that never last! The last one, only *three days lasted*, it did, gleamed OK magazine, super-smug, as usual. Ron, has promised to tone it down this time. He loves Vega too!

*

Mr Blobby's Theme Park is creepy indeed, as I was warned in Thursday's Time Off! That is why I am here. *I f tit* gets a bad review, I'm all over it like a dung-beetle; call it the undying reporter in me, the bastard in me, *if you well*.

I have dragged Ginger Biggles, here too. I didn't want to torture squid, Beepo, any more. He has suffered enough for the while.

Here, sat in the miserable kiddy's playground, eating our expensive Blobby-Burgers, he paid for drunk, seated at our unoriginal mushroom-seats, I leer at the children.

It feels OK to leer at the children, as they play. A big, fake Mr Blobby, pink and spotty hangs over us all, a tray of burgers dripping blood, giving us old men the paedophile-pass.

Paul Daniels, I wonder, and consider how many creative men came from Earth. I preferred Barry, his lad, who had a bit more hate and gave Deb's a hatfull of hollow when old baby-head did his final vanishing act. I am also surprised that Sir Paul, was never a paedo, or a killer, like Nasty-Noel-Redmond, and so I give him the Wizbit's pass to glory if he wants it.

"I don't," I chow down, making Blobby-meat bleed.

\*

Later on, on The Snail Trail, I had to restrain Biggles from reaching for a child in the snail behind.

"Get back in you drunk old bastard!" security yelled at him. They were already waiting as initially we were told by an attendant that it was kids only. Disgruntled, Captain Biggles had risen to the occasion, skipping over the fence and hopping us onto a spare Snail.

I shouldn't have followed him really, I consider, now, in the holding-cell, guards giving us dirty looks. "What a fucking idiot!" I tell him. "And take that hat off! You've spoiled my day!" I tell him. "Space-Raider!" I heckle him. "More like Gay-Vader!"

\*

"Orea-Mint-Chocolate is Fan-Tastique!" I tell Biggles, back in his rusty old space-ship, as he wrestles with the starter-engine, his cats in the back seat- Tiddles, Porg; named after the creatures he likes in the new-old Wars, movies, and other cats with random names of things he likes. One of those cats, a ginger one, like him, climbs onto my lap as the vehicle shakes with attempted life. It reminds me of Luigi, the thing on my lap; poor Luigi, who would in time fall from the window of my condo, far too high up to save any of his lives.

SPLAT!

BANG!

The old bitch is alive. "A-Ha!" he shouts, Ginger Giggles, kicking her into up-thrust like he's a boy-racer again, and she hates it but reveals her little-wings slowly, anyway. He clicks on the Jazz, fires his Eagle, slips her awkwardly -others beeping, cursing- into the vein, and I brace myself.

*

We arrive some shaky time later at The lagoon. It is very deep, artificial blue, full of chemicals as to keep it from becoming a diseased-soup when the beings swim in it on very hot days. Biggles has deckchairs in the boot, and gets them out, ready, and drinks. I tie a big hanky into all four corners, put it over the top of me head, give me vest a stretch-down over me beer-belly. I still have hair on me head, but it is greasy, full of dandruff, and smells, so gay Uncle Schubert, says wickedly, his sherbet lolly's he has always, to lure the little boys! Uncle Frank is still behind bars, by the way. When word got around he was still in cahoots with his notorious, psychotic brother, Bowser, he was investigated. Many skeletons were discovered and I wasn't surprised what happened! Some of the filth he used to send me on the phone, the sick bastard! The Underfoot Ripper! A distant Uncle of mine; I am not proud, and would have happily cashed-in had Holy-Wood come a' callin'. Yet, they did not, and I curse all my sick Uncles, blame all of my failure, and success, on them.

23

Writer – Wild Wilf Wilson
From June's Time Off!
2069

The Doom-Bot that has arrived here on Paradise 324, Planet Vega, *is incredible!* This is the Mark 2 version, brand new and ready for our collective viewing here at the 69' Boat Show, Day 1, at The Lagoon.

She has a dark, dark purple finish, and very much resembles Transformer, Generation 1 – Decepticon – Soundwave. Her evil eyes glow as she stands there proud, surveying us, and who knows what she holds inside her Tape-Recorder breast-panel, the size of a dustcart.

She is massive! And I dare to wonder for any of her victims, as I admire her Tech-4 Cannons and Rockets, her hefty Bazooka, the size of a Jumbo-Jet-Engine, in place of her left arm.

The crowd are excited, and so am I, as I munch on a hot dog as the disco-music ensues. Cue, spinning lights, action, as a chained space-cow is raised slowly on a platform. Oh the horror! As the Doom-Bot immediately incinerates it with her mega-man hand, leaving nothing but a pile of steaming barbecue, some taste, thumbs-up and cheer!

What a show! And neat tip-of-the-hat to South-African cow-killing-sci-fi-movie, District 9. There should be more inventive cow-murders in film, I consider, as the cameras flash and Doom-

Bot sparkles. Bruce, did flamethrower one in The Expendables 666, and then there was the bit with CGI Starscream, that cow, in Transformers – Darkest Of Darker Days 2. But then, I am an old man now, and still find pleasure at the memory of Bill Oddy, dressed as a beaver, shivering at that lake, yet, something about SC's new Law-Enforcement vehicle has me excited, and feeling safer -*than Oddy?*- here at rich-man's Vega, Day 1.

Rowdy Dog-Men, and *oddy's*, meet Doom-Bot!
5/5


24


4 Arc-Alien Avenue
TUA
Mars
11.22PM


I can't believe it! I'm back here this winter for a trip down memory lane, and a special report! Tucked up finally in bed I read the latest edition of Spookies, and it feels very appropriate here! After the Doom-Bot went nuts, we have all been *Emergency-Rescued!*

And I have been sent on a report by The Daily Space, indeed, they say be careful what you wish for.

The air in this bedroom smells of old paper; the room more of an old library anyway.

Old.

Gothic.

My new best friend, and wrestler - Richard The Nigger - as he is known, comes busting in, bare-chested, in his outfit, ready for more wrestling and cheap laughs.

"Not now!" I moan, as he grapples me, hoisting me above his

big, meaty, fatty tattooed arms, laughing at me then slinging me to the floorboards.

In a heap, crumpled, as he points and laughs at me, that young, cheerful face he has, knowing there will be bruises from that one, I distress at the mad idea before me.

Investigate 4 Arc-Alien, said the weird, drunk eccentric, Puffy, or whatever his name was, and there are five of us. Me, Mario, Richard, The Count, his Countess, and Steve-Oh! As he is known- a weird hillbilly-boxer with anger management issues, like The Count, and, well, all of us really.

It shall be a long six-months in this creepy haunted house, that is sure, and I'm sure that over that time all of our lurking skeletons and emotional issues will come to surface, and hopefully a ghost too, for Posh-Puffy, but mostly issues, I hope, mostly. Steve-Oh, doesn't believe in ghosts anyway, says it's bull. Maybe 4 Arc-Alien will prove him wrong, and we can all laugh at him when he shits himself!

\*

Breakfast is always a tense affair. Fortunately there are never many of us in this big, old kitchen, still good for gas, but no electric, strangely. I think the thousands of dangerous, fire-inducing black-candles, dotted around this morbid mansion, are here on purpose, to add to the feel and induce a ghost. Well, as I sprinkle milk on me flakes, it's day 3, and *I ain't seen nothin' yet*, I muse, worried suddenly I have brought enough of my medication to keep me alive?

Bah!

The City's a stone's-throw away from this desolate, rotting Sector, I smile, wondering if Salope, our sexy French-maid, puts out, as she bends over, checking the toasted cheese, her stockings very penis-stiff-inducing. "Toasted cheese for breakfast!" I moan to Steve-Oh, instead, taking my mind from saucy Salope.

"Fuck off!" he says, his flattened nose. He is grim in his thick dressing gown, cat-hair on it, from the cat he has at home, I presume, as I have not seen cats round' ere. He drinks black coffee, reads the papers. He always does this in the morning.

I leer at him.

I could have im', I wonder, unsure, as he is very large. Salope serves him his morning cheese toast, and I slide the ketchup bottle over to him, sarcastically, grinning.

"Fuck off," he says.

"You see," I say, continuing my story at him as he eats like a dirty bear. "In my dream, Savini's hairy, manly hand grabbed my throat, but the funny thing is, his hand accidentally went through the spike too, do you see the fun?"

"Fuck off," he says.

"I love my dreams," I continue, but judging by the hungover, hateful look in his eye, I shall wait until later to carry on my dream-stories at him.

\*

Puffy's sent us a fucking Boglin in a cage that morning, and Richard The Nigger, has already let it out.

Droglin, it is named; is dark green, quiet at the moment. In the Ballroom, at the bar with Salope, it watches me, big yellow eyes. "Say something!" I demand of it, refusing to poke it, or touch it.

Salope, seems wary of it.

"I wonder why it has been sent here?" I query. "There wasn't even a note, just a compliments slip from Puffy. Odd." I suggest.

"It's disgusting!" says Salope.

"Yes. There is something odd and repulsive about this little green one!" I concur, downing my SKY. "Fill us up would ye, Salope," I ask of her. "I'm gonna' get serious with this joker!"

*

A couple of hours later I was wasted. Salope, had long since retired to her quarters, and still, Droglin, just sat there. Occasionally it rippled, suggesting it was still alive, and wading through a big bottle of SKY, served to me in many shots by Salope, I asked it many probing questions, even threatened it with violence, once or twice.

Droglin, the little green bastard, is unbreakable, it seems. And, if I know these creatures well enough- they always have an agenda. This ones psychotic, unwavering silence is fascinating, and all of my reporter's wit and charm has failed.

Those horrid, yellow eyes, warty, rubbery green skin and claws. The way it just sits there, watching me, those unblinking eyes, full of...

Nothing.

And it was then that I slipped, as I went to get up from the bar here at the Gothic Ballroom, those candles flickering making the ghosts of the twisted former residents dance into the silent evening; *slipped*, glass cracked, and my hand came down on a shard as I attempted to steady myself.

Blood.

And, it was at that moment, that Droglin, sprang to life, fangs out!

## 25

Space.

2019

"Someone summoned Morgwar on Earth, Mathergaa! It has risen and killed them all!"

The Great Elder, regards his compeer with a wry-gash of a smile. "Fool," he cackles, his dusty cowl preventing him from revealing his eyes, for the best. "Did you not stare deep enough into The Orb? Did you not see D-Day, they unto themselves shall unleash!"

"I was told it was a rumour, Sire! Master Olsen, told us before he left!"

"Master Olsen is a trouble maker! And now, we win."

## 26

Jimmy-James-White-Black-Brown, lined his fat gut over the edge of the table, slid his stick between his fingers, narrowed his puffy, panda-eyes. The pink was in reach, and so was the brown, and White-Black-Brown also contemplated the blue.

The final frame!

And the air was tense that day on Paradise 324, the first Space Championship Snooker Tournament, Chav and Dave, there in the crowd for Jim, occasionally told to shut it! And yet again, an cyber-enhanced, yet, still gone-to-the-dogs, as cruel papers said, White, was a few shots away from the eponymous glory that had outwitted him for many, many years, much sullen drinking time, and wives, *and that smug cunt with the backward glasses!* He thought.

Now Space!

You can do it James! He whispered to himself, Rocket Ron, in the background, playing it cool, warming his hands with a hot pint of SKY.

Just a few more balls!

He could feel the eyes of an very elderly Jim Davidson, on him too, rooting for his geezer! Dirty Jim, his unending racism we all love and treasure.

And that was when something strange, freezing, and endly, passed through sad old Jimmy, his many names, folds, foiables, much-loved, and would be sadly missed as, Frame-Over, like his heart, it all gave out.

The crowd gasped!

Had they just seen a ghost?

"No! It was a shit-mist!" the referee pronounced, pinching his nose, as Ron, bothered to cradle the corpse of Snooker-Loopy-Jim, trying to look bothered.

"A fucking treasure, even though he never won!" Chav, would give the press later on that night at the bar.

"A few too many names though!" pumped-up Dave, cradling a blonde.

"Shut it!" Chav, gave him, raising his meaty, gold-ringed south-paws, that winked like the dirty Christmas record they made before they were banned from Earth.


27


I wake up!

Woke and never woke, and feel different.

I am in The Ballroom.

Empty.

Silence.

"What happened?" I ask myself, rubbing my neck, feeling the

wetness of fresh blood, seeing it, dark red in my hands. "That fucking Boglin, bit me!" I scream. "Help!" I cry, fearful of death these days as life is so good. "And now everything has yet again turned to shit! Bitten! Infected by a godless Boglin!"

"Oh! We have a God," it says, from somewhere near, a hideous voice that makes me tremble more. "Godlin. The thing is, I'm different! I'm a Droglin! Not Droglin. A Droglin! A vampire Boglin!" sneers the unholy imp. "And now, shit-pile, you're my slave!"

## 28

Albert, opened the letter with his letter-knife. His study was filled, a hoarder he had become, and the smallest crack of window, single-pane, allowed the fresh day into his tomb.

Dr Dragon Noir.

Tyr.

Finding his soiled armchair, wittled with black-mould, Albert, rested his reading-glasses onto his gnobbly-nose.

*Dear Albert.*

*What hides behind the eyes? Since 1886, I have searched for Count Dragoir, as you well know. The hoofbeats have indeed grown louder. A hand floated past, a ring glittered. I quaver in the light of my hearth, these days, old friend. My mind, tis not what it was. Lanblasted Apes! Outside my windows at night! Marshmallow people, their little fires in the sullen marshes, the blacke hours, their screams. From the highest pavement of the stair, my friend Thomas, once wrote, and now I get what he means. And I hope my words reach you somehow.*

*An invisible, eerie prescence, a stench of death was whence it began in the old house. Glad to be rid of that place! Back here, safe on Tyr!*

*I am not!*

*And more warm wee trickles down my leg in my fear and dreams of Granny. My knackers are clackers in the cold! An underpant condition, a bit of taut, elongated scrotum. Knee high boots, the beginnings of an erection.*

*Spunk!*

*A Dutch-Tug in Dutchland! A doughnut puncher in Deutschland! You see what this mad search has done to my mind, Sire! Warped her! Another sausage sandwich as another Space-Ape, goes by, incoherant mumblings, John Keats, an old friend, I wrote him many.*

*My Sergeant Sausage has stood to attention.*

*Another turf-chimp on the terrace outside.*

*In brief. I have lost it. And reming those people, and that idiot, Lord Huffstuffingpuff, to get out ogf 4 Arc-Alien, RIGHT NOW! SIRE! I emplore thee.*

*Sincerely gone,*
*Dr Dragon*

### 29

And it started *just that*, all over again, like Kile Reece, shat-out, all over again, chased by his old mummy's ghost, her hair of sharp finish.

I finished.

I, Mario Star, finished here, at the castle, on Tyr, living with a Wizard-Lord and Count of all Vampires.

Their slave.

Yet, it has its moments. And now I am a vampire, I get to live forever, and wander the endless halls of this fascinating, slightly miserable cosmic-castle, much like Castle Greyskull, on Eternia, a greenish, mossy, craggy finish, and skull-mouth door-well, where the victims enter having stumbled from the Forest Of Souls, very much like the same place in Mortal Kombat's Netherworld, those growling trees.

And it is a very strange, Gothic and heavy life we live here. Darius, his cowl with silver stars that shine, a glow from him, golden on good days, silver on days when he cares less. And the mysterious, wicked, sleazy Count Dragoir! Where to start! So many nasty secrets surround him, his gloomy dungeons, bats, the odd Vampiress, he chooses to keep alive, or Coffin-Creepers, as I like to call them. A Blood-Bimbo! I called one, once, and she bared her teeth at me with such wild ferocity, I immediately backed down like the dog I am! When provoked, I have noted, the Coffin-Creepers *hiss* like mother-Alien! It is terrifying- more terrifying perhaps than recent fire-works outside, in deep, deep purple space, where we are- Pink, too, and it can really send you mad.

Tis a place where time holds little value, the air, cool, serene, nonchalant, even in the face of nameless evil, Dragoir, brings to the table every day; the breakfast table, another one I have had to readjust to as things go seedy.

Sleepy now.

A belly full of blood.

\*

I am awoken by the sounds of a flapping bat, the windows

banging in the breeze, the long, silk curtains following the curves of the unexpected late-night cosmic wind.

What a strange feeling!

Was it the same one, Darius, whined about, tempting himself to write more scrolls, that golden cat watching him, cleaning herself in his ancient tower. I once peered over the edge of the window at that tower, and for a moment was flabbergasted at how high I was! Somehow, I restrained myself from throwing myself out, sacrificing myself to this unearthly, Space-Mansion of unimaginable ancience. "Whence once, ever a thing was as old as this place was, once," said Albert, the Butler, once a wizard, now happily retired, willing to make the tea. He was sent here too, by Those Gods! "And it is certainly not punishment!" Albert, told me one spaceday. "A man could happily live forever reading from the many libraries here," he said.

"But I have never found any libraries!" I had told him.

"That's because you haven't looked properly!" he told me, and for a moment his yellow eyes glowed, his black-monk's robe, beard of dazzle, straggle and such wisdom, said the others at breakfast when he wasn't around, which was often.

The bat finds her way back out the window, and I snuggle back into my new Vampire-life. That was when The Count, burst into my room, red eyes wide, beaming through the dark, his shadow taking the chamber. "We're fucking broke!" he screamed.

30

"This is a fucking disaster!" whines the count, claws in his hands, breakfast table, Albert, Eggs. Darius, says-

"Please. No more cursing for one day! For if it be true, we are in ruin! Say goodbye to all of our comforts!"

"What are you saying?" I ask.

"Silence! Slave!" glares the count, shovelling his Bran. I think one of the reasons he's soo skinny is certainly the fact he is long-time dead, but also his high-fibre diet that has inspired me. Being a Vampire has certainly cured my shits! No more projectile-vomit either! Ocassionally I vomit blood, if I drink too much, but...
"That we are down to minimal rations in everything, until Granny, curse her, wakes up!" insists count. "We must live like squatters, despite Our Majesty!" he screams, turning to mist, black, gone. He does that when he's really upset.

## 31

At first, I didn't take any of it really seriously, but after spaceweek three, or so, the seriousness, and misery of our new-found poverty began to kick-in, and the silence of the spacetime, took our friendship to new levels of tolerance none of us were certain we could maintain.

Granny's Silence.

That is what this abysmal time in space would, in time, become known as, and as I creep up the many brick winding stairs to Darius' Tower, I wonder how long this perpetual time will last.

A dead energy.

Nothing good going on.

Even Count Dragoir, has gone back to long hours of his coffin in the dungeons, killing the last of his hags so he could get some peace.

I fear for his sanity.

He wasn't very well, mentally, even before we entered Granny's Silence. Now he is down there, those cavernous tombs that run deep into these hills, connecting tunnels, carved right down, so he told me once, to the very Underworlde, where real Demons play, Dragons coil and witches and wizards duke it out! I should like to go down there, certainly now I live forever and have time. "What if I get ripped apart?" I had asked the count.

"Well, you get ripped apart!" he had replied, and I intend not to put it to the test. In my boredom, as this silence continues, and I step after step, upwards, a coil, a spire, I wonder that I shall need armour, if I am to go down, deep into the Underworlde. And a flamethrower! I muse, and wonder if magician Darius can magic all that magic up?

\*

"Can I come in?"
"Go away!"
"Can I come in?"
"By The Gods, you are wearysome, Star. Hang-on, I'm naked."

\*

"What do you want?"
"Well, I was a bit lonely, what with the silence, and I was wondering if you could help me out with an adventure in Hell, I had planned?"

Darius, swished across his study to the window, that golden glowing cat wasn't around, for once. "You should stay away from Count Dragoir, and The Underworlde, Star. I have told you many times!"

His voice was soft, persuasive

*

Nightmares, that night. I am taken back to the last days of my human life, Paradise 324, the day the Doom-Bot, went mad.

Oh the horror!

I am reminded in safe dream, HD clarity.

When Rumble burst from her Chest-Panel, Day 4, began crushing, great splashes of blood, guts; I knew we were in trouble. Crowds burst, literally into barbecue, as Soundwave, lost her shit. Not even Optimum's Prime could have stopped her wicked purple-metal-ass from the killing that was, en mass that day at The Lagoon. When Soundwave took her belligerent child, Rumble, for a walk down to the Kentucky Mall, even the army couldn't stop them.

Shopping bags of death!

Limbs everywhere! In the end they had to send in Godzilla, who moaned like the grumpy old amphibian-frog-mountain he is. He crushed them underfoot like sour, metal grapes.

32

The puzzle we play is quite boring, except for the prospect of the finished picture, that, thanks to The Count, shall be a naked human woman. On the TV, Dave Coppertop, the magician, makes another elephant become and areoplane, and all my spelling is fucked.

*Boogie-Music!*

I write randomly on my notepad, an old comfort. "The Forest Of Souls, is shockingly familiar," I tell Darius, The Count, Egg, the dog, there too. "I played many hours of Mortal Kombat, back in the day, on Earth, and felt strangely friendly with those scary trees as they growled at me this morning," I say, finding a piece of her vagina, making her vagina bigger, more complete- a black, hairy 70's rat!

"You should not wander alone in that forest!" Darius tells me, sincerely, his star-cowl. His glow has dimmed significantly since our poverty, *Granny's Silence*, card games, starvation, puzzles.

"What about that Magicke-Armour, you promised me?"

"You may receive that at Winter Solstice, should you be lucky!"

"It is Winter Solstice!" grumbles Count. "Haven't you seen the fucking snow outside? I hate snow!"

"You hate everything," says Darius. "Pour me another Brandy!"

"Pour it yourself, *Wizard!*" Count gives him.

Darius, pauses from the puzzle, a piece in his slender mystery-claw baring magic rings, huffs- "I meant Star!" and regards the lowly count, sighs, moves from the table, here at his Magic-Tower, *Study*, to pour himself another glass of the cheap red stuff from his final decanter before the booze runs out. "I suppose you two shall be wanting blood?" he queries, bending to pet Egg, that vies for his attention.

"And put more marshmallows on the fire!" says count, glaring at the very unfinished puzzle with beady red eyes, that have also been glowing dimmer in recent fathoms. *Still, at-least he has emerged from his dungeons*, I surmise, wondering whether the woman in the puzzle is a brunette, red, or if it is a trick of the light, or simply age, fading the printed image on the box-lid, we are slowly forming on table-top. Egg, scuttles over to me, sniffs my boots. "Be away with ye!" I tell the strange dog-thing, kicking him off. I'm still not fond of it, despite its friendly advances. Egg, can probably smell the weird mud I traipsed around in this morning, in the snow, where I found a puddle of steaming stuff that was refusing to freeze. I wallowed in that gloop for a while, listening to the trees growling in the forest, as the perpetual mist and drizzle did its haunt. Glad to be finally in Mr Cal's High-Tower, high on funny mushrooms, weed and fungus harvested from that strange forest out there in the inky white of this blacke place in the middle of space.

Hopefully the herbs will not run out.

The Count, sighs, as Coppertop makes something else massive vanish on TV, and Darius, makes Coppertop, vanish, as he taps the off button. "Let's focus on this puzzle," he says, seemingly unconvinced by that too.

## 33

George Washingmachine, woke with a start. He was naked, shivering, old, fat and fetal in the snow.

"You're awake!"

Through the gloom, cold, bewildered, George, turned to observe the cowering shadow near him; a shadow that had the familiar voice of a woman. "I'm freezing!" he shivered. "What is this?" he asked her, and her response was sullen-

"I don't know," she said. "I found you here, just now, like I found myself here, not long ago, and none of it makes any *ruddy* sense!"

He moved, shivering, sat up, felt sick as he felt a blanket go over him. "Who are you?" he asked her.

"Hilda Bates!" she exclaimed. "And you never came about that job you lazy old Baa'-Lamb!"

\*

Back inside the ancient hut, a fresh-fire going thanks to his new host, and old friend, Hilda, George finally began to warm-up. "This is madness!" he said, cradling hot tea she made him that he supped, spat-out directly. "What is this?"

"Tea, I presume," she told him, also wrapped in make-do rag-clothing, an old patchwork quilt draped over her shoulders, as she found seat near the fire, an ancient wooden chair, a small, hanging cauldron keeping water warm. "The jar I got it from had Tea labelled on it, anyway!" she said.

"The last thing I remember, was..." he paused, scratched his balding head. "I don't remember!"

"Neither do I," said Hilda, solemnly. "I just woke up here, right here, naked in the snow! I'm lucky I found this place!"

"Well, lucky you found me too, I suppose," he mumbled, unsure about that, taking more tea, finding it better than the first sip. "But what the hell's going on? Where the hell are we? And I'm starving!"

"A forest," answered Hilda, her ageing eyes serious in the gloom, fire-crackle of the hut. "A very *strange* forest!"

"I need some hard stuff!" said George, not able to enjoy the odd-flavoured tea at all, wanting coffee, with whiskey, a cigarette, some news from a radio that wasn't there.

Hilda, sighed. "I also want some answers," she said, as the *the* snow began to fall thick again outside the little frosted window. "I feel like I've gone mad!"

"Gone?"

At that very moment, a young lad, seemingly a human lad- pale, skinny, naked, wide-eyed and desperate came crashing through the door with a limp, startling the two older people. He eyed them once, with some relief it seemed before collapsing to the floor. A very fat young lady, also naked, clearly also panicked, half-frozen, followed him in, clearing snow from her pink skin, slamming the old door shut behind them. "H... Help us," she uttered, before also collapsing.

*

"If this shack is a Witch's cottage, I would have expected it to be made of cake and chocolate!" young, Sidney Melville pipes-up, warmer, also a cup of rancid tea.

"Yes!" exclaims Janice Fatterton, his Babysitter; still feeling bad at the idea, *mad*, for if what these old people have told her, she has effectively entered another dimension. What would Nora Melville, his mother say? And Peter! And she doubted her friendship with his older sister -Margaret, especially after her recent abortion- would last. "I'm just glad we're warm and safe! And, I never expected to see you out here, Mrs Bates!"

"Call me Hilda," she said, buffing her silver hair, strange not to be wearing make-up in company. Strange to not be in the Cafe today, too.

"I recognise you," said Sid, eye-balling old George, who hadn't said much, just sat there scowling, sullen by the fire. "You fixed our boiler, last year. Dad was furious! He said you didn't do it right, even after promising you would, he moaned to mum!"

Hilda, was smirking.

George, looked at the lad menacingly. "We may be in another dimension, son!" he said. "But a good smacking still works here, I'll bet!"

"George!"

"Oh, shut it!" he told Hilda, blunt. "Does anyone have any smokes or food?"

"I'll just pop down Tesco, shall I, George!"

"Get some cakes and candy while you're there," said Janice,

timidly, checking Sid's blanket was snug around him. The skinny lad had almost frozen to death out there! Luckily, Janice had some fat to keep her warm, and the blanket was welcome, certainly in the face of stark, revealing nakedness, she had never been comfortable with.

And madness!

"And buy a map too!" said Sid, smirking. "And a phone!"

\*

Violet, watched her human guests in her home from outside in the white-gloom and shadowy trees. Her claw gripped her long Staff -different in power to an ordinary Staff- and she mumbled things under her breath that only the enchanted forest could understand.

She had lived here on Tyr, in solitude, since Dog Star Days, a long time ago, when she was once banished from her former life as a Supreme-Sorceress on magic-fabled, Baboona. These were her first guests in some time- the first Human ones certainly, and the idea warmed Violet, somehow, and she warmed her home inside, from outside, with spells.

"Four guests," Egg, the Dag, said. He was beside her, her flowing dark-red shawl, an occasional companion when he was fortunate enough to escape from the castle. She looked at him with big, beautiful bright green eyes, almost cat-like, giving away her once Desert Cat Of Mars, heritage, many moons, lives ago. The little Dag looked quite pathetic in the mounting snow; a Dag, was very much like a dog, but a Dag. The cat-creatures here were not exactly cats either, but Cags, and they were one of Violet's first creations.

Cags and Dags.

"Four guests," she replicated in The Other, a more familiar language to her since banishment from her former Kingdom; a language Tyr, had given her.

"What are you going to do with them?" woofed Egg.

"I don't know," she said, feeling the feeling.

"You should go and see Lord Darius!" said Egg. "He'll know what to do."

"And I wouldn't?" Violet flared, her green eyes flashing bruised-purple that somehow frightened Egg.

"I wasn't being rude!"

"I should hope not," she said, sternly, knowing full well her terrible capabilities here in this forest- The Forest Of Souls, where, Violet The Cag-Queen, was The Keeper.

*

She had once had another name, a name that incorporated *Violet*, yet much of her former self was gone. Her long life on Baboona, The Monkey-Towers, seemed several lifetimes away, and though her life was very solitary, her only friends, the strange creatures of the forest, and growling trees, her powers had been growing for the timeless aeons that had passed since her *passing*.

Her time with the Monkeys gave her something- she took that something with her here, to Tyr. The fact she was Desert Cat, of origin, had left a strange imprint upon her also, one that had, in time, re-shaped The Forest Of Souls, to Violet's design. A work in progress, she considered.

It was one of her privileges, as Keeper, she had discovered, with time and immeasurable suffering, and still, she felt, the real reasons for her being banished here were undiscovered, unrevealed.

She had never met The Keeper Of The Castle, Lord Darius, and had not had good reason to do so, until now, she supposed, knowing that he would be well accustomed to Human behaviours, being the learned wizard he was. And that Castle, up on that mystic mountain, beyond these woods, was ill-fabled, crumbling, avoided in recent times. Cursed, some said. Violet, had avoided it over those countless moments on purpose, and-

Count Dragoir.

*

Hilda, was tidying around when Violet, entered her own home. All four humans stopped to regard her with bewilderment.

"It's Little Red Riding Hood!" pronounced George.

The woman in dark-red pointed her long, twisted stick at him, and suddenly, he found, his mouth was no more! He pawed at it desperately making muffled sounds.

"P-Please, don't kill us!" pleaded Janice, holding Sidney, tight.

## 34

The dirty puzzle was finished. Lord Darius, leant back in his seat unsatisfied.

"I wouldn't *have* her!" exclaimed The Count.

His ageing slave with plastic surgery, an *orange* finish about him, Mario Star, said- "I would!"

"Where is Egg?" Darius asked, out of the blue.

"He went out ages ago," said Star. "I booted him out actually!"

"I have that feeling, again!" mumbled Darius.

"Well, go use the en-suite!" said Count Dragoir, sharpening his claws with a nail-file, smirking an evil gash.

"No! It is a stronger one than that!"

"Maybe Granny's woken up finally?" suggests Star.

"Maybe? But I don't think so. This has something to do with the forest, and something else..."

"I was meaning to mention that," interrupted Star, eyeing his mud-caked boots, kicking them cleaner on the flagstaff floor. "I was down there, this morning, or sometime, and I found a patch of hot, bubbling mud- And, I stood in it!"

"*And?*" beckons the count.

"Well, it seemed strange... *Well*, strang*er* than the usual things I encounter in that forest. It was like..."

"Someone, or something had been there?" suggested Darius, glowing from his hood.

"Exactly! Something or someone important. I was meaning to mention it."

"And now you have," said The Lord and Keeper of the ancient cosmic castle.

*The Castle Of Death.*

"Who said that?" asked The Count, looking around.

"The wind," Darius told him, mockingly, leaving his Study in a blur, like it.

\*

As he descended through the winding stone halls, steep steps, giant staircases and corridors, Darius, noticed, on top of his empty stomach, how the effects of their recent poverty were firmly taking hold. Dust caked everything, the floors needed sweeping, barely any provisions left in the pantry, and still not a single word from Space. But, he followed his feeling nonetheless; it took him right down to ground level, out of the Skull-Mouth, across the moat and down the snowy path that went straight into The Forest Of Souls.

"A jigsaw puzzle!" he moaned, pulling his cowl tight as the thick snowflakes fell, the forest thickened, deepened. "A blasted puzzle from Earth! That is all we have had to do in recent time!" he complained, concerned at this time of Granny's Silence. "Not even a scroll to write, an order to send, any news to receive! And now, that odd feeling again."

He knew the forest quite well; well-enough to take a right at the first barely visible junction, a left at the next- but before long he realised that he was lost.

He allowed himself to glow brighter, warming him, shedding light to his surroundings, then studied the thick, foreboding trees around, above him. "Trees as ancient as The Castle Of Death," he exclaimed. "Why have I been brought here this day?"

And none growled, not even a face.

\*

Back in The Tower, Mario Star, poured his master a fresh glass of blood. "What's he up to?" he asked, Count Dragoir.

What with the recent blood shortage, The Count, looked paler, skinnier, more deathly than he had looked in some time. "He's chasing his *feelings* again!" he moaned, receiving the glass with a claw, allowing the rim to his lips. "With the shortage, the taste of blood had become very precious," he said, thoughtfully, allowing himself a slurp, then rested the glass on the table next to the completed puzzle, screaming suddenly in a manner that sent space-bats in the dungeons wild, as the glass spilt rich-red-blood, all over the naked human lady from the 1970's. "CURSE! A THOUSAND DREADED DAMNNATIONS!" were his terrible words that shook the very foundations of the castle sending Star, cowering into a corner of the mystic-study in fear.

\*

"What was that?" Darius, asked the deep-purple space of sky as the snow finally halted. "And what is this?" he queried, seeing the snow-hidden shack emerge, as he plundered deeper into the forest, following his feeling. "A hut! There are lights on! And people are home!" he said.

*

"So, this is *your* forest?" Sid asked the beautiful Witch, Violet, who was indeed beautiful, now that she had removed her red shawl and was stood over by the fireplace, watching the lost humans in her home with keen, big eyes, her bright white hair, long, where perfect ringlets found slender pale shoulders, perfect velvet pale skin. Her alarmingly green eyes regarded them deeper. She had allowed George back his mouth too, although Hilda, a motherly type had asked her to let him be- *all zipped up*, as she put it.

"Yes, child," said Violet. "I am The Keeper!"

"Where do you keep the fridge?" said George, obstinately, but instantly backed-down as she, and the others glared at him.

"Don't mind him, Miss!" said Hilda. "George Washingmachine! Our local repair-man!"

"Where is your *local?*" asked Violet.

"The Eagle! That's our local!" said George.

Hilda, huffed. "We are from White Lakes, Earth, as Janice said. We don't know why we're here, or what's happened..."

"Or where *here* is!" included Janice.

"This is Tyr," said Violet, softly.

"Tyr?" grumbled George, and Sidney Melville, suddenly sprang to life.

"No way!" he said, spiritedly. "I've read about here, I mean, Tyr, in an old space book! Tyr! The centre of the universe!"

"Some say that," said Violet, now warming her slender hands literally in the fire that perturbed them. "Others say the other side of The Other!"

"Do what?" grouched George.

"*The Other*," repeated Janice, pensively, having also heard fantastical rumours, being a lover of fantasy, science-fiction, fairy-stories.

"The Other," Violet, reiterated, smiling at the rosy-cheeked, chubby girl, in-fact, the Witch supposed, she had never seen such a large female human as the one now in her home now, but she liked her somehow, unlike the grumpy, fat old man, who said-

"This, that, or the other. I want to go home!"

"*That*, could be a problem," said Violet.

When Darius came in, the room stopped yet again to observe his mystic-majesty, black cowl with big, silver stars. When he locked eyes with the Witch, The Keeper of his forest, they both fell in love, instantly.

## 35

Six Time-servings later...

"I miss Earth, being human," whines Mario Star, paler by the day as the blood-shortage takes hold. "I miss TV, movies! Maniac Cop 2, Jaws 3, The Video Dead," he continues, not really enjoying the *Egg and Bacon pie*, Hilda Bates, from Earth, somehow rustled them up for dinner that evening. Since becoming a Vampire, Star had lost all taste for regular food, could barely tolerate it- Blood, was all he wanted, what he really needed, now, and those humans, the new guests were full of it.

\*

Out there in the freezing snow, the maze-like depths of the forest, Jimmy-White-Black-Brown, was frozen, naked in the snow, a lot like Laughing-Jack-Nicholson, in Ol' Stan's finest, The

Shining, those creepy twins and corridors of blood. A lot like Jack, indeed, except for *his* frosticle corpse was blubbery, very white was Jimmy-many names, The Snowman. Yet another test he had failed, and now, freeze-forever in The Forest Of Souls, he would.

\*

The Wizard, Albert, came bursting into The Tower. "Where have I been?" he asked, Staft in his claw. "And who are these humans? And why is there no food, the place a shit-hole?" he beckoned, sincerely. "Ah! *Violet!* Lovely to see you again," he relented, taking her by the claw and kissing it.

Lord Darius, head at the little table, a dirty puzzle covered in dried blood, looked up. "This is Hilda Bates, George Washingmachine, Sidney Melville, Janice Fatterton. You, of course, know Mario Star, and his Master, our illustrious, Count Dragoir, both of which slowly turning to dust as the blood runs out..."

The humans go suddenly tense.

Dragoir, eye-balls them. Water-balloons full of hot blood, he thought, vagina wet, penis stiff, in-fact, he really wasn't sure how much longer he could contain his twisted urges, needs.

"And it seems you know, Violet," continued Darius. "Well, she is my new girlfriend!"

"Really!" exclaims the old wizard, shifty black rags. "I'm delighted!" he beams, his yellow eyes and wicked, knowing grin.

\*

"Has there been any word from Golden Seal?" asks the wizard.
"No. Not even a purr," grumbled Darius.
"What the hell is this?"
"The last dregs of the liquor, Wizzy," says Star, drunk on it,

eyeballing fat Janice, wickedly. "We made a punch out of it! And, why can't any of you two just wizard-up some food, blood and drugs?"

"Granny's silence!" whines Darius. "Far reduced magical capacities for all Witches and Wizards at such times."

"You mean its happened before?"

"Oh, yes. Forever. Off an on, mostly when things go awry!"

"Oh."

"And this is a bad one. Real bad!"

## 36

*The Mud Monsters came from that weird steaming pile I stood in, that day, in the forest. They came from that gloop, and began causing trouble everywhere!* I write. *Although we have not bled the humans, I fear the current onslaught of Mud Monsters, may have em, should they breach the castle defences.*

*They are disgusting! Pooping and farting, all brown like healthy turds, yet sweaty in a way, slimy, and though slow, like Zombies, in number they are dangerous, and can overwhelm beings in their soil. And Violet, the Witch, tells us she was once human- a killer named The Kitty, in love with a Wolf! Does that mean that Darius has some of Mad Wolf within him somewhere?*

*So many questions. Soo much time. And now I think of that Droglin- curse the little green bastard, a thousand sick, twisted curses on his rubbery ass! There are a few Droglins here, deep in Count's dungeons where his ancient, oaken coffin with rusty nails rests forever, it seems!*

*He ain't gonna' die!*

*And it turns out, Chilly Nigger, was the lad in the Arsenal FC shirt, who found Mad Wolf's precious pocket knife, one day, as a child, playing football. He would go on to become a very big Gangster! A wonderful career, he had, did Ol' Chilly, those star glasses he would be remembered for, on Mars, Dem Niggas.*

*And where has Albert the wizard been? Darius suggested that he was lost for quite some time in the many libraries here at The Castle Of Death. Libraries I am still looking for, full of precious, forbidden books from all over Space. Occasionally, The Scaly Man, comes to visit us here at the castle, his Mobile Library Space Van, that travels Cosmia-Gallactic endlessly now, in spite of Granny's Silence, linking the cosmos in his scaly-way, a candyman of hope and wicked pleasures is scaly man.*

*The Count was pleased after having on reservation for aeons, the slim, notorious tome, Poems Dedicated To The Sea, finally fall into his claws, after scaly man's last visit. I got my usual copy of Man Mer, and shall his strange adventures until the end I shall never be graced. There is a rumour going around that Albert, is responsible for those comics. I wouldn't doubt it- he is a very mysterious old man, of very creative aura. I don't think he'll ever die somehow either.*

*I am no closer to my Adventure In Hell, either. With powers down, morale distant, I have decided to let that one simmer on low heat, as I still wish to do it, but I shall need many things, and companions, I have decided. Maybe the humans want to go to Hell? George looks as though he's been through it, well- they all do really.*

*Anyway. Nighty-night!*

## 37

"The mud monsters are at the gates!"
Pure dripping love fluids

And I am forced to finish writing as The Count, heralds the beginnings of a muddy uprise, against The Castle Of Death, her craggy, mossy ancient thick walls of sharp stone, her skull-mouth, draw-bridge of Why-Wood raised, mouth wide shut.

\*

"Let them try and get in!" I tell Darius, peering at the army of them outside, way down in the Castle Grounds, groaning, farting. "What a squalid, dirty rabble," I tell him.

"I wonder what they want?" Darius asks the Space, a desperate glow from him that is not reassuring.

"More importantly, how do we kill them?" questions The Count.

"I don't know. Get Albert! At once! And get the humans to The Keep!"

\*

"Flood the moat!" cries the wizard.
"You heard the man!" cried Darius. "Go pull the lever!"

\*

As the water from the risen water washes the last of the Mud Monsters, away, back into the forest beyond, we each fill our goblets with warm water to celebrate. It is a sombre affair.

38

That night, as the snow fell gently, stars twinkled in cloud breaks of fascinating shapes, Darius stood on a high balcony with his new /old love, Violet, found again, in time.

What a feeling!

He wondered, holding her again, the scent of her intoxicating as he ran his slender fingers through her fur. Her claws pricked up as he kissed her neck, and it excited him in ways he never knew, despite the poverty and silence.

Her eyes were bright green, his dark brown, almost black in that endless night that they stood there forever, arm in arm, silent. "Shit and squalor forever," he thought, utterly satisfied.

And they all lived happily ever after, until Count Dragoir, caved-in and drank the blood of all four humans in desperation, one dreaded evening they would argue about for aeons.

## 39

"What I wouldn't give for a Twinkie and a cheeseburger!" says Joe Don Baker, huddled in the corner of this deserted office block, overlooking the bay. The wretched bay- The Bay Of Decay, as the foul, melted purple imp called it on the boat here. "And a cold 888!"

Poor Ronaldo!

"Eat the crust off my dick!" says Goblin. "I'm already sick of this place!"

"Shut the fuck up!" Jack Jackal, tells him- The Undertaker, taking us all under, straight down to hell in this place. "I'm with Joe Don! Where are the luxuries?"

"Shut..." utters Kevin Valentine, fades.

"We should get out of here," I tell them, The B Team, *I*-Alexander Jones, poet, back for more. And the bombs, the destruction of the planet, all that. Certainly evidence, much morbid evidence of that here, where death and destruction also found shore, as we did, desperate, a long trip from Old-England, to here, France 2, as it is rumoured to be known now. Delta-Cal, the base nearby, and apparently we need to get there.

\*

In my dreams, I am him, Alexander, whomever he is, I write. Me, Mario Star, I remind myself, remembering the recent batch of starvation-induced-hunger-mares, that were very cruel-

For in those, I was in Harry Potter's class at Hogwarts! A right, smug little sod, he and his ginger mate, and the one that never puts out, being uptight and posh! God, it was a dull term, as some old blad, bald nightmare, piped-up in the shadows, pages of trees, books later, glowing little mall rats; I am glad somehow to have sat in Miss Rowling's class.

She balled me out a few times in her office, rat-faced, tight-lipped, and I nearly cried, for laughing- though I love her enthusiasm, like little Harrys, I told her, before she told me to get out!

Back in class I catapult another sticky ball at Gwendaline's head, hoping to get her attention. But much like dull, goody-goody Harry, she refuses to have fun as she practices the dark arts, glossed over!

What a lot of nonsense, I wonder, and put me boots back up on me desk to annoy the support, Miss Coppercunt, wife of Top, and just as mystic, as a plank of wood.

A glue-ball finds Harry's head, and I cheer, laugh and point at him as I leave the classroom under familiar instruction. "See ye Harry!" I tell him. "I'll be waiting for ye, in the broom-cupboard with all the other old sticks. Tell mummy I still love her," I remind him, winking at him, leaving the room, doing the Fonz.

God I hate school!

Take me back to Ghoul Island, where the grass is dank and the girls are sleazy..

\*

Back in Hogwarts, I eventually get friendly with Slithern, whom seems alright. "Got any dope?" I ask him.

"Nah!"

"Here, go on, tell Gav he's a black bastard!" I prompt him, and he giggles. I like Slithern. "I like your hair!" I tell him.

"Thanks," he says.

"Now, seriously," I tell him. "I can get you Potter's dick on a stick, if ye want it? But, I need to know who sells the dope around here, kay?"

"Deal," he says, and I maybe better off in this new term as the bell rings for old Professor Fufflecakes, hilarious cosy tea-time-wasters!

"A bit a filla'", I told Esmeralda, another posh little stimpy, who scowled at me, and I nearly grabbed her arse. Instead I did a wanking gesture at her and her token Asian mate, chubby, cock-blocker! "How do you spell VIRGIN?" I asked them, and Slithern was there to share their sweet pain as I whipped em'!

"Fuck I need dope," I tell him.

"I'll get you some, Star, you dick-less little shrimp," and I like his words.

"Get some cigarettes too, and booze. Lots of booze. Forget spell-books, wands and all that shit. Focus only on drugs today," I tell him, very seriously.

*

Quiddick!

And it sucks!

Sucks like old Mrs Brown on a Sunday, ten-bob a pop. A lot of hard work, so I get baked and watch em' all from the sideline. "Go on Slithern!" I cheer, unbothered, but on his side as he scored me weed. I also get to look up Esmeralda's skirt, get flashes of her knickers, and it takes me off to the toilet where a wank was inevitable.

Thick globules of spunk, all over the floor, I marvel. Quiddick! I wonder, doing me fly. I hope nobody slippick in that! I glee, cracking a can.

Back on the sideline, satisfied, finally, I sit in the grass and slurp a praise in the direction of Rowling, as I eye her, cheering. I look at her for a while, taking her all in, knowing I will be wanking to her later on tonight in my dorm.

40

My name is Shithatty Sambo! I play drums with The Nice And Nasty Quartet, a bunch of ex-roadies, who play prig-jazz really well. And tonight we play for Rotunda!

Queen Rotunda!

The good grace of close friend, our Boss, Chilly Nigger, his pet dog, Wolf, his Casino, we residence, most nights, Dem Niggas!

We god Dave Miles, on the horn, Shaggy, on the electric guitar, percussion, and Slimy Sapphire, on the Double-Bass, and boy, do we kick it!

"They can kick it!" Chilly, told TV, recently, here on Mars, MCC, where it's all at! And we did, that night, too, on, Jewels Holland's Music Show.

It seems us old black boys have still got something to show em, humming to myself, rehearsing lines, licks in my mind before our performance tonight, alone at the bar, where I like it, pre-gig, a shot of Bourbon, or six, a cigar, soak up the atmosphere, see what we're dealing with.

It is the science of Jazz!

Dave Miles, got it a long time ago, back in the days Jazz was new here on Mars, rougher times, times of woe, starvation and poverty. Racism was a pretty big thing back then too, and we all wondered if we might survive.

They had us picking space-cotton from the fields where there is now a giant Urban Lagoon, and that was where me and my boys learnt the sweet, soft relief in Jazz, as we hummed and sang, and boogied all day long to kill the backache, heartache and abject misery.

\*

It was in the pulling of the cotton-storks, the plucking, that I learnt the subtle rhythm of the drums, and I played them all day long, yes I did. I liked it in the background, holding up my fellow-pickers, and felt better there keeping a steady pace, avoiding the whips. One day Skipper, got me, and I felt the cruel lash of that twelve-tail on me bare, black back. "Friggin' Honky!" I gave him, and he whipped me again.

"Pick up the pace, blacky," he told me, and I will never forget his cruel eyes. In songs these days, such as, I Was A Lowly Cotton Picker On Mars, I hit the drums extra hard as I picture his face, Honky-Skip, his wonky hips, shuffling behind with his thick whip. The long, long fields of cotton, the long days there on that alien planet. It was our brotherhood, our music that got us through those days and somehow I am grateful for the pain. For without such pain, I may well not be the focused, seasoned drummer I am today, and I have forgiven the whips and white hoods of creepy clans. When the shotguns and Lazers rang out during the revolution, I was there too, and today those shots still ring out, all over me skins!

Every night we kick it, live at Chilly's Bar, glistening with splendour, smoke-machines, lazers, balls, the lot. Space beings from all over the Universe, converge here every night to gamble, cavort and jig on the dance-floor; Pink Camel, his friends. Their wild dancing pushes us to our limits, and rumours are they will be following us here tonight at secret Rotunda's, show us support. And we may need it judging by the faces of some of the drinkers, gamblers, thieves and villains, here tonight. But I like the spinning ball, and there's something good here in the bad of The Underfoot Arena, *oh yeah!*

\*

What a wild place Mars City Central, is! It has changed a lot throughout the years, we all agree, and this place, Queen Rotunda's- this place has never changed, except tonight we get to play, The Nice And Nasty Quartet.

All four of us have been roadies, around Mars- that's how we met- not really the cotton fields, yet I was a slave there. Dave Miles, a pianist, turned horn-blower, Sax-Master, Trumpet-S*c*pecialist. Slimy Sapphire, his Double-Bass of woe and jig. How he finds those notes, those *beats* I shall never know, and we clicked instantly on our first eponymous jam. And then there's Shaggy, a Thumper and Blues guitar, sleaze-breaker, breaking into wiry, sparkling-sonic solos at given quarters. With a bandanna laced with LSD, he's high all the time, and psycho-trippin' like Hendrix, a lot, does he do with that old, beat-up guitar he cherishes.

What makes our Jazz, is the nice *and* the nasty. Each of us can bring some turbulence to controlled surface, following each other's nerves, patterns, ways we know, songs we never tire of. It is a slick, creaming-machine, ice-cool, our outfit, and many wonder we should be Universe famous, as each of us could have been, had that been an issue- As it is, Mars Famous is plenty good enough, the mad crowds of multi-different specie fill out the halls for pimped-out-Jazz, every space night, popping champagne, taking drugs and catching the notes, the crazy musical notation this Planet's biggest, bustling City, is famous for in Cosmia-Borealis, The Gallactic!

And that shall indeed be the name of our next record-

Jig Gallactic

Where things get meaty-space, and we're gonna test some of that out, right here, *tonight!*

\*

Sadly, It was on that ghastly night that I, Shithatty Sambo, died, after an invasion of Dog Renegades, that terrible night. I woke up, having been blown-away, in a strange forest, freezing, dense and white. I headed for a castle in the distance, and it was in that castle that I found, Darius, Star, *Dragoir* and Albert. Four very strange cats.

Their French-maid, Salope, let me in, black-bollock naked I was, that wretched night, pounding at the giant door. She eyeballed me, let me in, and after getting wasted with them all that first night, I realised, that despite the fact I had lost my life and everything, that I was also in the company of another bunch of mad Jazz-cats, and set about writing a list of instruments for the wizards to magic-up.

## 41

On Friday the 13th, I, Mario Star, discovered a wardrobe in one of the myriad bedrooms. Through it, for whatever chance, I was able to walk right back into haunted, 4 Arc-Alien Avenue, but only as ghost. The drunk, The Dag, and The Wardrobe, I would entitle my new mystery novel, based upon my adventures back to Mars, that haunted house. Some of the things that happened to me were so far out, even I wondered if they were real, so for a while, as I went often into that magical wardrobe, I kept a journal.

*One day, in 4, I met another ghost, a pink one, all flappy-wide and pouty like the pink-nintendo-sponge ball. But then I realised that it was, in-fact, an hallucination induced by MMD, the latest drugs all the kids are taking, and some has found its way to us here at The Castle Of Death.*

*The house, No. 4, is generally empty, in-fact, I have yet to see any other ghosts than myself, and Egg, who sometimes comes here, Ghost Dag; and I wonder exactly why there is a wardrobe here at the castle that acts as a portal to Mars, and makes one a transparent, floaty ghost. Yet, one can not go out of any of the doors or windows, into the streets, and I have tried!*

*Another mystery, riddle.*

*4*

*Like Chimp Biscuit, our new band we have yet to start, that newcomer, Shithatty Sambo, keeps banging on about. I'm not sure Sambo's all the ticket, to be honest! I think he might have punched-out on the crossover, here, Planet Tyr. Still, he's keen, and it's nice to have another blood-bag human in the castle, just in case of another emergency shortage, or Granny Silence! That was unbearable, the last one, where we all nearly ate each other alive, and me and the count drained the four, poor earthlings in desperation one evening.*

*Wild desperation! I must add.*

*We had made a pact, not to drain them of their blood and kill them, certainly the younger ones. Yet, sadly, it is true, as Count, promised it would be. The youngest, were the best! Though, their screams will be long, long unheard, very sadly.*

42

Tyr is like a giant nipple on a breast. The only Island on Planet Tyr, and The Island Of Tyr, is the only Island. Sea covers most of the planet- turquoise, magic seas of azure madness.

My room looks out over all this!

Castle Grounds.

Forest.

Beach.

Sea.

In a perfect rings, all around our hill, like a nipple.

"I am the only one who knows the secret," says the bearded old man on TV, in a cave. "It's incredible!" he says, and I smile, knowing that I know the secret too. I also know, because I have seen this particular movie many times, that this poor old gravedigger -or coffin-dodger- is about to meet zombies, and be eaten alive!

Yes! I even have a TV now, flatscreen, wall-mounted, Netfix, with a surprisingly good reception, and a bunch of Blu-Rays, mailed cheap via V-Bay, from Earth.

I'm all set up to live forever now-

"And now they're setting up a strange laboratory!" I tell Egg, laying on the bed with me this space-afternoon. "Dr Cleaves, the Dalek, his crew, all out in that new metal eye-sore, Area 69! Who knows what they're getting up to out there?"

\*

Snooze.
Dream.
Hogwarts!
Haggard!

"You little shit, thinkin' you're all tough!"

"Make like Jackson, and Beat it, Bigfoot!" I tell him. "Hanging around with little children, playing kiddies games, acting the giddy-coat, all cuddly, really covering the real you, a drunk paedo!" He starts to throttle me! "C-Choke on H-Harry's little dick!" I gargle.

## 43

Mario Star is exceptionally drunk and high in The Tower, that day-

"They wanted it full barrels, so I gave it to em in Brokedick Hilltop, me last book! Ye! That was the one where I said that *I the* person I want to fuck and eat the most is Dora The Explorer! Still is! Ye! Her little monkey. Now I'm a vampire I'd probably just drink her blood!" I stagger.

"I never read Hilltop!" says Shithatty Sambo.

"It's the one where two gays go up a hill and come back down cured. Very controversial! Pride wanted me head on a rainbow, they did! I told em they have to git in line, after Dora, and Rhianna, was was also in Brokedick. She played bi-curious coffee-girl at bottom of mountain."

Darius sighs.

"Ye! Now I've got a new book in the mill- The Drunk, The Dag and The Wardrobe. It's about the mysterious magic wardrobe I fell into while exploring rooms, like Dora. Egg was me monkey. Ye! Staggered in, and found a load of dust, space and a big haunted mansion the other side that makes ye a ghost, like Nicole pale Kidman, in Others. Ye! The other day I haunted pest control! Dressed up in one of Salope's dresses, like ice-queen; Egg, made him the Lion, then gave em the Spookies. Sadly, they didn't see me and just did their jobs instead. So, not much to go on at the moment, just wardrobe, and a new cross-dressing habit, I wanted to come out about," he says, dropping his trousers, revealing knickers.

44

1

One Day, Peter Doughatty, turned up at the castle door, giving it all that. "C'mon man!" he whined, and I took my time, watching him through the door-hatch, post-hole, bit, where Pete, shivered, naked as the snow fell on him. "Let us in man! It's bloody freezing! I think I've snuffed it!"

"You look like a Skeleton, pal!" I told him. "Are you sure you're not a skeleton in disguise?" I ask, concerned after recent Skeleton troubles.

"Na! I'm a human mate! From Brighton fella! Let us in ye cunt!"

"Alright, hang on! I'll go pull the lever, but you'll have to stand back. Or, I could send down a bucket, if ye like?"

"Who are you, anyway?" he asks.

"Mario Star, at your service, lost one. Butler! And this, is The

Castle Of Death!" I *Th*espian.

"Well, open up Greyskull and let in Prince Adam," he says, and I wonder about this Doughatty, who shares a similar name to drummer-Shithatty, yet, is pale white, like the bleached-bones of a fragile Skeleton, unlike Shithatty, who is black, very black.

\*

"What finds you here, young Sir?" I ask him, having wrapped hippy-Peter, in a woolly rug, large enough that he may cover his meagre intimacies. We make the long ascent to The Tower, where before our wise, dark council, I shall *po port* dubious Peter.

"Death!" he says. "An overdose! Right after Brat Anderson did his! He ain't around here, is he? He owes me hundred nicker! Suede! He'll feel the leather o' me Brighton boots, should I see him again!"

\*

In The Tower, they were playing playing Cricket, as usual. "Ha! They do this! The Wild Bunch!"

"Botham's got nothing on me," says the wizard, lining-up his bat, ready to receive the dangerously heavy red ball from The Count, who rubs it into his crotch, leering and grinning. As usual, Darius is umpire, and stands behind the three indoor wickets- he raises his hand, to stop me and Pete, in our tracks, and I notice Salope, is fielding, by the bookshelf, bent over, beautiful cleavage sagging out, wobbling as she shuffles near Egg.

Count, bowls his wicked overarm-demon-spinner, grunting at

his back, but the wizard is indeed a fine bat's-man, and takes it plum, clack o' the sweet wood, the smash of another window.

"Six!" declares Lord Darius, drunk and drugged as shit, it seems, as they all are, I know, as I was with them earlier at the Hawaiian Bar, downstairs, wondering what activity we were going to play today. Cricket, has been popular recently, but the broken windows, some precious stained-glass are fewer and fewer here in The Tower, his Cosmic-Lord*hip's* study, that is starting to resemble a shit-hole again, the first time in a thankfully long-while, since the last dreaded Granny's Silence, a Cosmic condition, very frustrating, like Cricket, her intricate and many, many rules, like Rugby, and all English games that are complicated on purpose, to add to the stress of the game.

I love The English, their Empire and Chips.

Shithatty Sambo, is having nothing to do with it. "I prefer American games, Baseball, Basketball..."

"They've recently got a new Blood-Sport on Cable, inspired by American culture- High-School-Hategasm!" I tell them, cause' I watched it last night. "The kids fire real hate at each other in a maze of corridors, and flamethrowers! The most hated of that week's selected School are the Aliens, armed only with guile and battery acid in the teeth of their costumes! The popular ones, full of hate, are armed with flamethrowers and go after em! It is clearing the overcrowding problem in Schools significantly, and the kids love flamethrowers, acid and aliens! It's great!" I declare, my arm around confused, half-naked shivering Pete. "And then there's the new one on IT3, Immigration Sharkpool! You can guess how that works!" I beam, wondering about my own hate-levels. "I love TV," I say. "This is Peter Doughatty, by the way!"

"Hello, Peter," mumbles Darius. "Right! Last over!" he says. "Then tea at the bar."

\*

At tea, with SKY, Peter, explains how he comes from Earth, was once a famous rock star with a perfect Egyptian girlfriend, yet, sadly, in the end, both did themselves with drugs! And there is something about the little skinny human- English! Indeed!
"Weren't you English, once?" I ask Albert, the wizard.
"No. I was under British Law. I was one of the Atlantic Claws! But, yes, technically, I was English," he says, reloading his pipe.
"He's been all over the galaxy!" I tell Peter, a Brighton Chav, who is warmer, and looks quite good in the Peter Pan, costume, Count, has leant him.
"*Leant!*" Count, reiterated. "That means *borrowed*, and no blood, piss, semen or faeces stains! *Yes!*"
"And where is this place, again?"
"Tyr Island, on Try, I mean, *Tyr!*"
"Oh."

\*

Peter settled nicely into his new death here at the castle, me, the new Butler, it has been decided, and so I have donned an appropriate suit, and now live in the rafters, with other bats, spiders and fodder. I have also adopted a creepy gait, to add to my Butler, role, here at The Castle Of Death, where most spacedays I attend to cleaning and cooking duties. Fortunately I have Salope, here to help me and leer at, and so my life here at the castle, living-dead-vampire-and-Butler, is not as bad as I thought it might be.
I've still got me Netfix, up in the beams, nailed to a sloping

ceiling, very poorly fitted and dangerous, as it hangs right over me coffin, where I lay and look up at it. And it can be awful cold up there, in the winter, two years having passed since my arrival here, having been slave-shipped by a Master-Droglin, that green one, that bit me; cold *as the death* that imp gave me that day, night, drunk, back on Mars, many moons ago it feels, that fucking haunted house! Cold! Like the snowy winters here on the island, the seasons, similar to those on Mars, or Earth, the Earthlings, Peter, and Sambo, tell me. Two blood-bags, both Count, and Myself are unwilling to drain. I fear the black one has HIV, the white one AIDS, and we are well taken care of now with regular deliveries of Blood, via the Blood-Van, a concept created by vampires, much like the legendary milk-van, that does the rounds, it is, except blood.

Hang on!

Shithatty's from Mars! I wonder, remembering his constant abuse stories. A damn fine drummer though! He has set himself up, at the grace and magic of the wizards in one of the rooms, using it as a practice studio. We are all in the band, but are not very good yet, or commited, as Sambo, moans about a lot too!

Chimp Biscuit!

A right shambles, except for brilliant Sam, and Pete, who is also a musician, he says, and is good as he wails like a baby and hammers his guitar like a spindly-punk! "Can't stand me now!" he yells, and it's true- some can't. So, these two, as you can imagine, are the core of the group, and we all just make more sweet noise around them.

I had an electric guitar once; Les Paul, limited edition, Figgy Shitdust, King Edition, bright purple, authentic cigarette burns and hot-spoon indentations. There was even the little marker-pen tag, Suzy-Q, a heart, with a needle through it, teardrops- cost me a small fortune, but looked good in me posh condo on Vega, Paradise 324, I miss quite a lot- human, happy daze, gone.

*

"Kiss, kiss Molly's lips," Count sings at Salope, seducingly, slinging his claws at her, but she's having none of it.

"Beat it!" she gives him, indeed, Salope, though saucily-seductive, and French, is no easy touch. "Sus ta mere!" she says, giggling, filing her neon-pink claws, a new claw-colour, she has chosen, as she has changed the die of her hair and is bright-blue at the moment- a goth-clown-sex-doll! Though I don't say that, and wonder what she said. It sounded scathing, and Count, recoils, scowling, his creepy, tight black Italian suit, slick hair, dark jewels and dead ways.

Dye!

The Tower, here, is tidier, after Cricket, that lasted for some days, and a house-warming that went on for quite some cycles too, to welcome Pete, was the excuse, although each of us here at the strange, magic castle knew that it was alcoholism and drug problems that made the non-stop party of these early days, better days, before the very dark and light days; not that newcomer Peter, minds. He's been trying out all the exotic mind-menders we have here, and Violet, the Witch, Darius' witchy girlfriend, back at her hut is busy drying Shrooms, recently harvested- the best – 4.

It's all good! And young Doughatty, can't wait to try em' out! Especially after our wild stories from last year's harvest. "They were nuts! *4 is the nuts!*" I told him. "Count, thought he was Egg, Egg, thought he was me, I thought I was everyone, all at once whilst Darius, puked from the window, high and stomach set-free, as a freebird into the night!" I gave it. "Salope did the exorcist spiderwalk backwards up the walls, and... well! What a night! The wizard even became a witch, and flew out of the window on a broomstick, cackling like an old woman! Or that my have been the MMD? That reminds me! Come on Pete," I bother him, dragging him by the arm. "Let me show you the magic wardrobe in room 4, Level 4! It's wild *mate!*" I say, like he would/does, trying to bond, get him to see my Wardrobe, as no-one else is remotely interested at all in it.

*

Things went too far during latter-days of bonding with Pete, as the Cricket set came out again, although this time, woe, as Egg the Dag, was killed by a screamer, sweetly struck by The Count, who is not only good at bowling, but batting too, it seems! Egg, was out in the fields of *study*, with me, Pete, Sambo, the wizard and Salope. The bastard was deep into a century attempt, when Egg, tried to catch another clacker with his teeth, and the hefty ball took his head and teeth off, *out* and all over the wall.

Cried, some of us did that day, as joy became so many, many tears.

*

The Great White Sasquatch, or He, as some called It, came to planet Tyr, one Winter Solstace, it did. It came by broken Space-Ship, The Hi! Ho! Silver, hoping to land at Cleave's Hanger 69, but was told to piss off! By a rather obstinate Dr Cleaves, that day. So, he bothered us at the Castle, that day, instead, he did.

What a beast!

As he stood there, nine feet tall, suitcase, glowing white, thick Bigfoot fur, his Space-Ship, behind him, smoking, very dirty, He, having travelled some distance, it seemed, said- "Can I get a room here for a few night?"

As Butler, I regarded him disdainfully, as one should the creatures of the backwoods hills, forests and mountains. "Hmm," I noised at him through the hole. "What's your business!"

"I am The Great White Sasquatch!"

"And I'm a gay uncle!" joking, but wondering if it were true for a horrifying moment. "Hang on! I've heard of you! Lord Darius, spoke once about you, and none-too favourably neither, it should be spoken!"

"What did he say?"

"He said you're a troublemaker! Like The Godfather, among Sasquatch."

"That may, or may not be correct, stranger! Now, let me in!"

"OK," I said, opening the big door. And, in too came, Pink Camel, who had been hiding, to my surprise! "Sambo's mentioned you!" I said, greeting it, allowing them passage indoors through her majesty's massive skull-mouth, fearsome and very uninviting. "Pink Camel! The breakdancing legend! I never thought I'd see it with me own eyes again! But this is the castle of death," I weary. "And anything may or may not happen! Come on in anyway! Let me take your coats and weapons."

\*

And so, with everybody in, as Shaman-Jim, once screamed, it all began again, like Chucky, his dolls. The Great White Silver Sasquatch meant night*s*, not night, as I suspected, yet, his bulk, teeth and bright white hair, glare, startled us all into allowing him refuge. It turns out that *He*, and Pink Camel, his best mate, are on the run- a John Wick, deal, he said. And He knew that Lord Darius, being the quite caring, famous, trustworthy, generous and stupid wizard, would allow him sanctuary from all the many bounty-hunters out to get him.

*He* bonded with Sambo, immiediately. "Good to see a f*ee*low brother," he told him, oddly, as he is a very white Sasquatch, and Sambo, a black cotton-drummer humanoid.

Darius doesn't seem very impressed. He sits scowling at the window, probably waiting for his girlfriend, Violet, or Golden Seal, the wise, curious glowing cat from deep space he likes too.

Albert the wizard watches us all. "Can I have a word with you, your Lordship, in private?" he asked.

\*

"What are we going to do with him... It. *He*."
"I don't know? Having him here is dangerous!"
"I agree."
"But it is He!"
"Yes. That is true."
"We should be careful."
"Yes. Very."
"Yes."

\*

Twas on day 4, the day after Egg's sad funeral, that something strange happened at the castle, for as each of the residents awoke, ready for another day of jinx, bubble, play etc, they each realised that they had been robbed! The wizard, lost magic scrolls, one of his collectable wands; Salope, her frilly silk knickers, lace-bra and expensive jewellery; Star, his porn, a few Blu-Rays and some weed; Sambo, nothing; Peter, much drugs, drinks, poems, and worst but not least, Darius, and The 5 Magic Rings Of Evil!

He was fucked! And so was the universe if he didn't get those precious, dark-magic rings back from thieving bastard, Silver, his cunning mate, Pink Camel.

After emergency council, with Golden Seal, it was decided that the search in space would begin immediately, an incredible bounty for the recovery of Silver Sasquatch, He, Pink and the 5 Rings of evil. Then...

That very meeting.

Monday Morning.

A Raven, pure carrion-black, razorbeak, perched on the crumbling window-ledge of The Tower. "Eat shit!" it said, then flew off.

Twas a purple morning, of Fallen, orange leaves falling, ominous omens, shapes, patterns, halloweeds, and noises from the heavens, all around the orb it twas. It may well have been Summer, in-fact, it probably was as the seasons tended to fluctuate as the day went on. The purple vacillated between deep, shallow, mauve and flashes of pink, wondrous but deadly pink- and in that liquid paint splurge- red, blood red, a dapple, dash.

\*

Space-Parrots, unimaginable colours in distant, many suns, King-Sun, the biggest ball, their wings in their many winkly-eyes, of fire. Such were the new-morns, new-born every day on perfect Tyr- A big, hairy nipple, as Count, called it, not realising how lucky he was, losing nothing to the thieving claws of dastardly He, and Pink-Camel, and his comfortable life at the castle he was often very ungrateful about.

In came one of the many new pygmy-small brown servants, a bit like an Ommpa, but shipped in from the job-centre, his uniform, chosen by Count, a silver, skintight jumpsuit with their allocated number printed on their little backs. "I bare word, My Lord!" he bum-licked, having only just got off of the banana-boat, and still feeling the slim remnants of renewed hope here at the castle, his strange, new masters, planet.

"What do you bare?" Darius asked him, smoking Wok-Weed.

"I bare news, Sire! It seems that He, and Pink-Camel, have not even made it into space! For their ship has been found crashed at the beach, My Lord! Local Marshmallows said they saw his ship come down, smoking from the jets, fucked-looking, My Lord! They crash-landed at the beach and were seen scampering into the forest with loot, Sire!"

"Good work, silver one! Now! You and your little friends go play in one of the rooms, now, and let us big people do business, OK? Oh, in-fact, prepare the cages in the prison quarters ready for so-called He," he says, waving a claw. "Ah! I can see her now! My sweet love! Here she is! Coming out of the forest! My Keeper! *She* will know best how to find and capture He, his weird mate, that fucking Camel!" he said, choking heady smoke.

\*

"Come on! Get up ye lazy bastard!" Violet, tells Darius, waving her Staff at him, and even that hasn't worked.

"I'm couch-locked!" he moans at her. "Damn Wok-Weed! Very fruity, and there's the Formula One Hundred, on today. Mickeschumaker Shumaki, might take the Cup? It's the Baboona 100, too, love; yer home Planet, or something? Come and sit down my treasure! Our treasure will find itself, you'll see!"

She looks at him sideways, bright green healthy eyes, unlike his, dull, blood-shot, and he's not glowing like he usually does- so many drugs and toxic things recently. Maybe he does need a rest? She considers, being a reasonable cat, but- "Get up out that armchair!" she shouts instead. "And get the guns out!"

\*

Traipsing around the forest that day, the hunters stalked their prey. They found the wreckage of his vehicle, The Hi! Ho! Silver; the billowing smoke gave it away, and friendly Marshmallow people, who knew Violet, well, showed them the way through the dense woods to it. Sadly, The Great White Sasquatch and his breakdancing villainous wolf in camel's clothing, had taken their loot with them to wherever it was they were hiding. Grandpa Marshmallow, said that they were seen heading north, or south, but to the other side of the island, anyway, and though his information was little, and quite useless, it was better than the usual gibberish the tiny Mallows gave them.

\*

At a calm lagoon, the other side of the island, The Castle Of Death, lights left on, in the distance, up a mountain, the hunters, weary of traipsing through the psychedelic forest, set up camp for the night on the psychedelic beach. The serene, azure ocean lapped at the sparkling soft-sand-shore, the air sweet, and each of the gang were weary from the day, drugs, dancing, jokes, and once again, happy for the soothing ocean as the suns went around early, for it was *Fallen* right then. The Silver Slaves, set-up bar, loungers, generators for the disco lights, music, smoke-machines, party-poppers etc. The others made a big fire, got it going, then settled around the long bar, while Sambo, did DJ, spinning soulful C.Ds, and Star, cooked fish-steaks on the barbecue, a sweet-spicy marinade, a big silly hat, apron with plastic titties.

Lord Darius and his Queen, Violet, did nothing to help, but sat there, on their special deck-chairs, being regal, grinning, enjoying the sunset together, their eyes locked sickeningly. The wizard, didn't do much either, instead smoked his long pipe, gave out orders, and complained once or twice to Star, about keeping an eye on the steaks, catching them right. "I miss Egg the Dag," Star whined as the suns went passed sea making night, and real stars, and he fumbled with his spatula, did the plastic humanoid one, a Star-Lord, nonetheless.

"Stop crying, keep cooking!" the wizard told him, prodding him from his seat with his Staff.

\*

"Well, night one of the hunt begins!" declared Darius, saluting us all with his Goblet, his guests at the beach, drunk, stoned, three-courses in front of them, slowly being served by the slaves. "And may it be a very merry one!" he said, saluted Space, as if those Rings Of Evil, meant nothing, the havoc, destruction, chaos and *Evil* they would cause were they not recovered. "In the words of the Great Lord Sauron, of Middle Earth... Party down!"

\*

"There are a few things on my mind," the old wizard tells the older *younger* one, the party settling down, everyone settled around the fire, the ocean, soft, reticent in the background, the blacker hours.

"What?" asks Darius.

"Dragon Noir. Morgwar. The 4 Problem. And these rings..."

"Worry not, old friend. Dragon has lost it, we have lost Morgwar, rumoured to be in cahoots with Godzilla, in Space, and The 4 Problem; Well, we have a team of top scientists working right away over at Area 69, I am informed by Dr Cleaves. The final, fourth chapter of Von Rancour's book 4, is being cracked as we speak too, at Brainchester University, on Earth, no less!"

"*He*, stole the dark-magic book, Poems Dedicated To The Sea, too, The Count, told me earlier!"

"*He*, probably liked the cover! Very gruesome! It is of no concern! He, knows not what he has, and he has nowhere to go!"

"*We*, can only hope!" says Albert, pipe-on, serious, despite the lovely beach at night. "And what if Morgwar's on his way here? You know he has ancient beef with the Elder Keepers of this castle!"

"Bah!"

"And what if he turns up with new pal, Godzilla? What then?"

"Hmm," noised Darius, Violet asleep in his lap, purring; he, feeling suddenly also more serious, re-lighting his own pipe. "That is only a whisper!" he said.

"No! Golden Seal, said it!"

"Oh!"

\*

A Space-Whale cries her haunting sound across the ocean

somewhere, her many blow-holes, the bag-pipes of the sea- where the noise carries across the island, right across to the other side, the same beach, but the other side. Sat on that beach, in the darkness, not even a fire, He, and Pink Camel, pulled their treasures around them to keep them warm. "What are we going to do?" shivers He. "This was your f'kin idea!"

"Me? You're John Wick, mate, not me, boss! And now, we've stolen sacred treasures from a mystic castle, and that does involve me, I suppose?"

"All of this involves you, Idiot!" grumblegrowls The Great White Sasquatch, not at all fond of beaches, but the sand is warmer there, and softer than the forests or mountains of this odd place in the middle of space. "Right down to all the recent dodgy deals- you're ideas!"

"You can't blame me, boss! I'm just under order!"

"Don't give me that, Camel! You get paid the most, so that means you're my number 2!"

"I never thought of it like that? I always thought I was The Jester, doing me breakdancing, all that?"

"Fool!" moans the big Silver He. "And now those wizards and witches are going to turn us into shit! I'm glad we didn't steal from Shithatty! I liked him!"

"I tried to steal from him- his C.D collection! Some very rare stuff in there! But he woke-up and I ran!"

"Fool! And to think I let you fly!"

"The ship was already fucked, boss! You know that! That's why we had to stop here! Lost in Verboten!"

"That was your fault too, two-humps! And now we're going to be either eaten, killed, raped, tortured, caged or magicked! RATS COCKS!" He yelled as a space-crab bit his Bigtoe. "Once I was King Of The Hill! Now, I'm a dead flea-bag-bum-on-a-beach; Driftwood, with nowhere to run and an idiot pink camel for a friend!"

"Life's a beach," joked Camel, and He, kicked him with his Bigfoot.

"Get some sleep!" He moaned. "First thing tomorrow morning we build a raft! And let's hope the village idiots don't get us before we set sail! And if you see any more of those marshmallow people, net-em' in Salope's stockings! Can be eaten raw or roasted! Both ways good!"

"There's coconuts, too!"

"Yeah, well- you can get your gangly, pink hairy ass up a tree, in the morn too! We can drink their milk!"

"I have water in my humps!"

"Pass me the knife! I want my share, Camel! I want one of those firm, pink back-titties you got for a water-sack! And any more lip, or spit, and I'll be using that fur of yours as a rug, as I cross the oceans, eating your corpse, using your skull as a toilet-bowl, your four, long, pink dancing legs, as oars!"

Pink-Camel, kept quiet. When his master's insults became vile and life-threatening, which was often, Camel, had learnt to just stay quiet. The Bigfoot, were known for their foul temper's, and this one, the king of em', once, was a prime contender for rage-release and wild fury! Indeed, He, was not known as The Great White Sasquatch, for nothing! Although he was old now, and Pink Camel loved him.

\*

The next morning, Violet, kicked both ageing animal-gangsters awake- kicked sand right at em'! "Wake up losers!" she said. "And no sudden moves or I'll turn ye both into sand, like this beach!" she said. "Sand!"

"Just don't let the vampire on me!" whined Camel. "Please!"

"They've already gone home. They don't like morning. Who's this?"

There was a man, a naked, skinny old man, laying next to the Sasquatch and Camel, their stolen treasure; Violet, prodded him with her Staff; he woke with a start. "Don't kill me!" he cried, clearly bewildered, face like a skeleton, a very bad comb-over.

"Another soul?" asked Darius.

"Clearly," said Violet. "Who are you old skinny man?"

"I... I am Peter Brandon Samuel Milk! Number 55, and I killed Serene Dreamone, I did! God help me! I killed The Angel Of Love!" he wailed, clutching his face in despair.

"The plot thickens," says Albert, raising an eyebrow, yellow eyes reflecting the yellow-pink-purple sunrise happening slow.

"Keep your eyes on these three! If they make a move, change em!" says Darius, expression hidden, as usual, beneath his cowl, never giving anything of his handsome face away. "Gather the treasure, little ones, and bind these three scallywags! My hangover this morn is a cancerous bollock! And I've just about had enough! Butler! The paracetamol! Slaves! Chariot! Star! Wine! To the castle, we go!"

\*

And just like that we were all safely back at the castle of death, where the Ommpas lead the dastardly trio, in chains, to the dungeons where they would await trial and our treasure, including the 5 most important rings in the universe, were safely dished-out to their rightful owners.

Later on that day, when things had settled down, I snuck into their holding cells with a spear I found in the magick wardrobe/house and big surprise for one of them.

"Fuck off Mario!" they whined, as I poked them with it.

"I'm The Butler!" I told them, enjoying their collective misery. "I practically run this joint, and a little bird, I mean, a glowing golden cat of infinite wisdom, informs us that you three have all had it coming! You, Silver Sasquatch, for your gangster ways, murder and serious crime; you, Pink Camel, for fraud, aiding a Boss, riot-inducing breakdancing skills, being pink; and YOU! Mr Milk!" I give him, spearing him enough to make him scream. "You killed thirteen-times, Whammy-Gold-Award-Winning, singer/songwriter, Serene Dreamone!"

"I-I was out of my mind! I..."

"*Tut Tut!* The Dark Council Of The Tower, salutes you, Sir! And you shall be released immediately. Great White and Mountain-Back are to rot here, in the dungeons until further notice!" I sneer, removing the big key that will allow psychopath-reporter, Mr Milk, into our union, here at the castle and annoy the other two even more.

Click.

The creak of a cage door.

I take my time.

As Mr Milk's little, skinny, getting-old-man's body scampers from his cage, I prod his back again with my spear. "You dirty little man!" I tell him. "Can you play cricket?"

"You bastard, Star!" says Silver, at the bars of his cage. "First you hunt us, then you cage us, nothing to eat or drink for hours and this creepy little nut-job gets the green-light!"

"And Cricket!" adds Camel, his hoofs gripping the bars too.

"Nighty-Night!" I tell them, flicking off the light for them. "Sleep tight. We're off to the bar for more," I goad them, slamming the iron door shut behind me, pausing both me and mental Mr Milk, just for a moment-

A sweet little moment as they screamed in the dark, and cold, *and I* shivered, though not with cold, but with warmth-

The warmth of their suffering, for it was indeed, The Great White Sasquatch, who killed my buddy, Silver Buckstar, back in the day, the great white hairy bastard!

*

Nightmares!
Hogwarts!
Haggard looks at me. His eyes are bright-red, narrowed, droopy, done. In his maw, the big joint I rolled us.

"Better?" I ask him.

"Yeah! Thanks Mario! I was taking life here at Hogwarts all serious, I was! It's Miss Rowling! She's awful demanding! And then there's her chain room! And the kids these days!"

"Her what?"

"I mean... nothing," says Haggard, drawing another killer hit. "Where did you get this anyway?"

"Slithern! He's alright, despite his hair that looks silly really, even though I told him it's good," I wonder aloud, dream-baked. "Harry's alright too, I suppose! He has the best hair out of all of us and may well bang Gwendaline!"

"Aye! Little four-eyes! I love him, he's a good lad, a lot of promise!"

I look at big Haggard seriously. "Not *love* like *that* though?"

"Like what?"

"You know- the ol' boy wonder meets bear scenario? Tell me the rumours aren't true!"

"Listen! There are always bad folk here at Hogwarts, spreading their baddies! Especially these days! But I am a goody and have never banged nor abused none of the children, I tell ye!"

"Alright! Just checking. It's the way our generation is and were made- paranoid, nosy, pro-active, annoying, judgemental, positive, Evil, selfish, lazy, callous, ambitious and weak. It's not our fault, Haggard! We're snowflakes, generation X, Y Z etc! Virtually useless and fragile and fickle as dust. In-fact, please don't heckle me with your hate-crimes, Sir!"

"Do what?"

"Pass me the joint. Your hate-crimes, for being nice, and my feelings! They are tender, *tinder!* A need for social justice, peace and harmony at any costs, and always a safe-space or a man-cave to socialise online in safely, yes!" I giggle sarcastically. "Freedom, equality, modernity! The feeling I should become a woman after years of vile abuse at the hands of them. Yessir! Cut me dick off and paint me black! Take all me money and wee-wee on me from high up. We, the nothing, *for* the nothing, all brainwashed and bullied into believing many, many things, more, and all that! And that, Haggard, is one of the many reasons why I love school and living everyday with other humans, their joy, and need dope, to prevent me killing meself, every day!" I glee, pleased with my meandering hate-speech.

"I'm confused."

"You will be," I tell him- and slower: "You *will* be! Welcome to the new-age, old-timer! More crazy than a box of frogs, *word-salad* and more serious than 1984, ever predicted. Thought crime! Old boy, in this new-land *everything* is a crime!"

"Give me back that spliff," grumbles Haggard.

"Still, at-least religion's quickly flushing away now, thank God! That old chestnut! And the rise of The Satanists! Hail Satan! Except, I am a bit *bio*-confused, me Ol' Haggard- for not is it religious to believe in the good Lord Satan, who is needed for balance, it must be said? And, you see, I don't believe in anything! Not a single fucking thing, never have. Yet, they seem a lot more *party* than the new-age goody-goodys, they do, the devil-worshipping ones."

"Oh?"

"And that makes me bigger than the devil, you see," I glee, stoned, very stoned, knowing that The Angel Of Death, was now upon the sickly humans on Earth and hiding on Mars etc, and how I always found partys overrated, borderline pathetic and desperate.

And all other gay, puritanical or uber demons, dicking around like they're it. Like they know!

The Angel Of Fucking Death, I wonder, high and very warm, deep inside where my heart is carrion-black and I know the bright-white secret, *her* blessed, black wings unfolding, smoking the dream away, the cold, hard truth of reality, kicking-in and *ass* all over this silly, perfect joke of the Universe.

Knowing.

"And not giving a single fuck," I relax, falling to sleep, in my sleep, being very friendly with The Angel Of Death, the big bird.

That was when Ted X, the most intelligent voodoo teddy in the universe got on stage, all smug on me laptop screen.

Everyone listens...

"Go fuck yourself," says X, calmly, leaving the stage.

Best speaker ever on the subject of life, I comment, giving him a thumbs-up.

Printed in Poland
by Amazon Fulfillment
Poland Sp. z o.o., Wrocław